Unexpected Gifts

Ariana Gaynor

Romance Novel from
Dragonfly Publishing, Inc.
www.dragonflypubs.com

UNEXPECTED GIFTS
Romance Novel

Hardback Edition
EAN 978-1-941278-26-0
ISBN 1-941278-26-4

Paperback Edition
EAN 978-1-941278-27-7
ISBN 1-941278-27-2

eBook Edition
EAN 978-1-941278-28-4
ISBN 1-941278-28-0

Story Text ©2015 Sherri Good
Cover Art & Illustrations ©2015
Dragonfly Logo ©2001 Terri Branson

Published in the United States of America by
Dragonfly Publishing, Inc.
www.dragonflypubs.com

DEDICATION

To everyone who's ever gotten a second chance and went for it.

CHAPTER ONE

FLAKES swirled and sparkled in the soft yellow glow of the security light like glitter in a shaken snow globe. Goose bumps, which had nothing to do with the cold, peppered her flesh.

He floated five foot above the snow accumulated on the lawn.

"Why are you here after all this time?"

"For you."

"What do you mean, for me?"

"You...alone...." The distance and wind carried most of his words away from her ears.

"I can barely hear you. What do you mean me alone? Because I'm alone?

The light dimmed, and he seemed to gain strength.

"You shouldn't be alone," whispered past her ear on a breeze that never brushed against her skin.

She automatically took a few steps backward when he appeared to glide closer.

"A little late to worry about me now. You left me a long time ago." Grief squeezed her throat, making it hard to take a breath.

Sadness pinched his features. "No choice. I wanted to stay forever. But things can't go back to what they were, we can't go back to what we were. You need to move on with someone you can love, until we...."

His words fluttered away into the air as the light brightened and he faded.

"Our boy will come around. You will find love again. I promise...." echoed in her head as light filtered through her closed eyelids.

Flinging a forearm over her eyes, she wanted to go back to sleep. No reason to hurry out of bed, except the deadline her editor imposed on her. She'd not missed one yet and didn't plan to miss one now. These dreams were starting to affect her concentration, though. She relented and crawled out from under the covers before her subconscious raised a ghost of Susan, the slave driver who never let her slack off.

Thank God for coffeepot timers.

She quickly shrugged on her fleece robe before the morning chill soaked in too far. Following her nose to the kitchen, she grabbed the crème brulèe creamer from the refrigerator and doctored her coffee just the way she liked it.

Sarah Wilson nursed her morning coffee as she took in the view outside the large picture window. The sun rising over the mountains in the distance never disappointed her. She remembered the last summer she and Rick spent together, back when the cabin had been their vacation home and the only place Rick truly loved to spend his downtime. He'd wanted to stay another week or two, but her publisher and editor needed her back for several meetings. Now she regretted not staying the extra week.

Memories of Rick and their son, Chris, sledding over the hill and the snowball fights they enjoyed in the snow-covered meadow, chose that moment to come flooding in. Memories of her and Rick enjoying a glass of their favorite wine in front of the fireplace, of sharing their morning coffee, watching the sunrise as she did just a little while ago.

Things were so perfect back then. Her writing career had finally taken off, Rick had received a great promotion, and they were having a wonderful life raising Chris. In the next instant, Rick lay in the hospital wired up to every type of machine imaginable.

Chris moving in with Rick's parents after the accident, so Sarah could spend more time at the hospital, had been a relief. Chris wasn't comfortable being at his father's bedside all the time, but she couldn't stay away. He needed his routine to be as normal as possible. He continued to live with them after his father's death, blaming her for letting him die. She'd spent hours with Rick's parents discussing the rift between her and her son, and they tried their best to help Chris understand his father did not wish to be kept alive with machines. In the end, nothing did any good. He'd cut her out of his life completely.

In losing the love of her life, she lost the second greatest love of her life, her only child.

She never imagined life without Rick, or that Chris would cut her out of his life. Yet, here she sat reliving the past completely alone. Why couldn't her son see the things she'd done were what his father wanted? Even so, the responsibility of removing Rick from life support took every bit of strength she possessed. Would Chris ever understand and forgive her?

She shook off the memories and noticed a sudden squall kicking up as she focused on the here and now. At least the storm waited until the sun rose, allowing her to enjoy the morning's first light like she used to.

She rushed to her room and threw on some jeans, her flannel shirt, and heavy socks. This storm could easily turn into the blizzard the weatherman had been forecasting all week, so she needed to get the firewood stocked. She grabbed her coat and gloves from the closet and slipped into her insulated boots. She loved a roaring fire, a necessity for Montana winters. When Rick had been alive, they never stayed through the winter. Only for the first couple of snowfalls so Chris could see and enjoy the fluffy flakes before going back to California.

As a kid she'd loved Montana winters. The entire family counted the weeks till break and their ski vacation. Those were some of the best times of her life.

The wind blew cold air straight up underneath her coat, chilling her to the bone. "Damn, it's cold." She filled her wood hauler as high as the bin allowed. Thank God, she'd found the wheeled cart online, promising to make moving a fair amount of wood in one trip on days like this possible. So far, much to her relief, the promise held true.

She unloaded the first cartful and headed out for one more.

Sarah looked toward the mountains, but the heavy, thick falling snow quickly reduced visibility to nothing.

The hauler fit easily through the door and slid in beside the fireplace without taking up a lot of space. She stripped off her coat and gloves and hung them by the door. Her boots were next. She untied the laces and pulled the frozen monstrosities from her feet then placed them by the fire to dry the faux-fur cuff around the top. After stoking the flames and adding a couple small logs, she headed for the kitchen. Time to warm up with her favorite spiced chai latte and a light lunch of a grilled cheese and ham sandwich and tomato soup.

She gathered her notebook and pens, setting them on the table with her laptop as the teakettle heated up. The snow continued to fall outside while she watched through the kitchen window and let her mind wander.

The snow fell hard and fast as she watched from the warmth of Westmore Ski Lodge.

"Hey, you, what are you doing over here all by yourself?"

Turning from the window toward the voice, she looked straight into Frank's eyes. "Hi, Frank. Where's Alan?" Frank, her first true crush, was her brother Alan's best friend all through high school.

"He's over by the fireplace hitting on a couple girls." Frank grinned at her.

Her brother's flirting was legendary.

"I should have known." She laughed. "Why aren't you over there, too?"

"Not interested—"

The kettle's shrill whistle interrupted her memories of the ski lodge and the night she began to think Frank might have feelings for her. Too bad she never found out if those thoughts held any merit. He left for college that spring, putting an end to her hopes. Her only link to Frank was secondhand stories from her brother.

She prepared her latte while the soup warmed and the sandwich toasted on the griddle. Before she knew it, memories of Frank pushed to the forefront again. "Why do I keep thinking about Frank? I've not heard his name in, I bet, ten years."

She'd gone on to graduate high school and get through college, which is where she met Rick. They were in love, but the emotion never matched what she held for Frank in a tiny corner of her heart. She'd chalked her first experience up to a case of puppy love and told herself nothing would ever seem as perfect as her first. Rick stood the test of time, been her rock, and the love of her life. Married by twenty-three, she gave birth to their only child, Chris, two years later.

Chris was fifteen when his father passed, robbing him of everything his father had to teach him, robbing him of a father's love and support as he learned to be a man. By her fortieth birthday, she'd lost her husband and her son in one flip of a switch. That was five years ago—five long years of rejection from her only child.

She'd cried so much in the first few years, there were no tears left. Nothing remained but a heart crushing pain when she thought about the family that came and went too soon from her life.

Sitting down at the table, she finished her lunch only because she knew she needed to eat. Her appetite soured long before her food finished cooking.

Maybe now would be a good time to revive one of her unfinished romance storylines.

A couple love lost and found plots scribbled down in an old notebook came to mind. She could bring someone back or kill someone off. Not that she ever killed anyone besides the occasional vampire or rogue shifter.

Thankfully, her writing had never abandoned her. She'd always been able to lose herself in the different worlds she created—lost in time and space, being the creator and destroyer of all her imagination conceived.

Once she cleared the dishes, she put the kettle on for another cup of tea.

She fed the fire, grabbed her grandma's quilt and placed it on the sofa, then went back for her cup of tea when the kettle whistled again.

Hoping to get some writing done, she curled up with her paper and pen. With the cozy quilt and roaring fire to keep her warm, she soon dozed off without penning a single word.

* * *

A pacing figure emerged from the mist.

"Damn it! I'm never going to get the hang of this being dead stuff. Every time I try to make myself visible, I can't. All I accomplish is making her remember events from her past but not all the things she should. I can't even make her hear me until she falls asleep. Why is this so hard to get a handle on?"

"The way she's shut herself off from everyone and everything isn't healthy. At least she's still writing, when she doesn't get too comfortable and nod off, which is so typical of her."

"Rick?"

"Hello, love. I'm sorry it took me so long to get back to you. There's a lot more to this spectral stuff than people think."

"Rick? How? You're gone. You left us." She scanned the misty ether surrounding them, trying to make out familiar landmarks. "What is going on?"

His eyes revealed his regret as she went through the emotions of fear, longing, heartbreak, and grief all over again.

"Calm down, honey. I just needed to see you, to talk to you. I know what Chris is doing and I want you to know I'm taking care of everything."

"Oh, Rick, I miss you so much. Chris is so upset with me. I don't know if anything will repair our relationship."

"I will take care of Chris. But right now, I need you to stop hiding from life. There is more for you than this half-lived existence—more love available to you."

"Not for me, not without you."

"Yes, without me. We will be together again, but in this life you need to move on and find love again, for me, for yourself."

He began to fade before her eyes.

"I hate this part, it makes me feel like I'm falling apart cell by cell. It's one major creep factor besides the entire being a ghost issue."

"Rick, don't go, there's so much I want to say to you."

"I can't stay any longer, but I'll be back…in your dreams."

* * *

"RICK!" Sarah startled awake, sitting upright and reaching out to an empty room. Realizing she remained alone, she flopped back down on the sofa and threw her forearm over her eyes. Rick seemed so real.

Why now? Why dream of him now after all these years?

The clock on the oak mantel chimed four. She'd slept through most of the afternoon. She wished her nights were that peaceful. The naps didn't help much, but seemed to be the only time she rested. Well, used to be, if this latest type of dream continued it would put a stop to what little sleep she did manage to find.

The quilt lay pooled on the floor, it must have slid off her when she jolted awake. She bent over and picked it up. The smell of Rick's favorite cologne tickled her nose and disappeared just as quick.

"What the hell?"

My imagination must be playing tricks on me.

There was no way Rick's cologne had gotten on the quilt. She'd received it after his death, when her grandma passed away just a couple years ago.

More memories of Frank and cuddling together in front of the fire after snowball fights in the yard at her childhood home bombarded her. Then thoughts of her and Rick sitting in front of the fire at the cabin once Chris went to bed after a day of skiing filtered in.

She had to keep busy. These trips down memory lane were getting stranger and stranger. Nothing specific happened to bring them on. No crises or calls from old friends, they just randomly popped into her head.

At least the snow had stopped. She moved over to the window to see how high the drifts grew after she'd fallen asleep. Only a slight dusting fell while she napped, but the sky continued to look ready to dump another heavy load of flakes.

After a quick dinner, Sarah bundled up and went out in the cold to stock more wood in case the blizzard hit during the night. She walked out to the shed and checked the generator. She'd learned her lesson the first winter alone at the cabin with a small portable generator. Having the larger liquid propane generator installed, with two large propane tanks the gas company filled every fall, was the best improvement she'd made. Her tub held second place on the best improvement list.

She stripped off her coat, gloves, and boots for the night and headed for the bathroom. The double-slipper, copper tub called her name. If a blizzard was coming, she wanted one hot soak in before the power possibly went out.

Her favorite bubble bath filled the bathroom with a heavenly lavender scent. She wrapped her hair in a towel, so she didn't have to deal with the blow dryer before bed. As she slipped into the tub, the hot water and lavender relaxed her tired muscles. Maybe she'd be able to sleep tonight.

Once she cleared her mind, time slipped by without notice.

I really need to look into a hot tub. This water never stays hot long enough.

The wrinkled skin of her fingertips and the lukewarm water let her know she'd been in the tub too long.

Dressed in a comfortable pair of yoga pants and a t-shirt, she walked into the living room, grabbed her favorite button-up sweater, and wrapped herself up in it.

"Sarah."

"Who's there?" She searched the empty kitchen and moved down the hall, looking into the guest bedroom. No one hid there, not in the closet or under the bed. She flipped the blue dust ruffle back down as she stood. "Come out and show yourself," she yelled. Moving into the next bedroom, which she used as an office, she checked the closet—empty. She cleared her bedroom and the bathroom. She was alone in the cabin, so who whispered her name?

"Wonderful. Winter is just getting started, and I'm already getting cabin fever."

Back in the living room, a nonexistent breeze ruffled the corner of a sheet of paper. The page contained the scene where her latest hero and heroine meet for the first time. Her mind raced thinking up what created the breeze—a draft, heated air from the fireplace, a ghost, maybe Rick? He had been on her mind lately, especially in her dreams. "Good luck going to sleep now."

Walking back into the kitchen, Sarah filled the kettle and set it on the stove to heat water for tea. Tonight was perfect for the Tranquil Dream herbal tea she preferred when sleep eluded her.

While she sat at the table waiting for the teakettle to whistle, she jumped at the sensation of someone playing with her hair. A tear slipped down her cheek as she sensed someone palming the back of her head. "Rick?"

Rick always loved to play with her hair and palm the back of her head while she rested against him in the evening.

She'd never believed in ghosts, but her opinion was

changing. Too many coincidences had presented themselves lately. Rick in her dreams, various memories popping into her head, hearing her name, and the sensation of Rick being near again. "What do you want from me, Rick?"

She jumped when the water in the kettle boiled and set off the shrill whistle.

Sarah laughed at herself, stood, and walked to the stove.

Great, now I'm talking to a dead man. What a way to keep it together.

He died five years ago, so what made her imagine him now? Was she that lonely? She didn't feel she was, but apparently her subconscious did.

Surely that's it. Rick wouldn't wait this long to haunt me, right?

Chuckling at herself, she laid her head back on her shoulders and stared at the ceiling.

I think my imagination has run away with me.

Standing and stretching, she decided everything she'd imagined was a direct result of being overly tired.

The big wrought iron canopy bed sitting in the center of her bedroom beckoned her. Maybe with the aid of her tea, the soft pillow top mattress and the warm down comforter would once again be her island of rest sans dreams of the past.

She kept paper and pens stashed throughout the house, never knowing when inspiration might strike or a character would give her a good one-liner. A notebook and pencil laid on her nightstand, waiting for her. All she needed was to slip into her favorite fleece robe, grab her mug of hot tea, and crawl into bed, writing anything that came to mind until she, hopefully, fell into a dreamless sleep.

Looking up as she turned off the overhead lights, she saw the snow falling in large fluffy flakes outside the kitchen window once again. The storm finally arrived.

Intent on reaching the sanctuary of her room, her steps faltered when a loud pounding on her front door interrupted her calming thoughts.

"Who in the hell is stupid enough to be out in this weather?"

She listened for another knock to be sure someone was truly there.

Bang, bang, bang!

She jumped at the strength of the knocks as she set her tea down and grabbed her Taser from the hall console table before heading for the front door.

Bam, bam, bam!

"Hold on, I'm coming!"

She left the porch light on out of habit, but when she peeked out the sidelight of her front door, the electricity flared and then went out. "Shit!"

A flashlight flared to life outside as she rummaged through the drawer of the stand by the door for matches. Thankfully, she filled her oil lamps the day before in preparation for the possibility of this exact thing happening. After making sure the lamp stayed lit and the security chain remained engaged, she slowly opened the door. The next thing she knew she was looking into the ice-blue eyes of her old friend, her first love, standing on her porch covered in snow.

Clearing the snow from his clothing, he wasn't paying attention to who opened the door. "Sorry, but I ended up in the ditch trying to get to the lodge. Can I use your phone?"

"Oh my God, Frank Taylor? I didn't know you still came up to the lodge. What are you doing here—out in this mess?"

The mention of his name got his attention. The smile that spread across his face brightened the now dark evening. She closed the door enough to disengage the chain then swung it open.

"Sarah! I thought you were in L.A. or somewhere like that."

"I used to be in L.A. I've been here for two winters now. Get in here before we both freeze. We can catch up later." She stood back, laughing as he entered. "Did you not check the weather report before you left your place this morning?"

"Thanks, and no, I've been on the road. Before you ask, I spent the drive listening to some new CDs I'd bought just for the trip. I knew to expect some snow, but thought I'd make it back before the storm hit. Guess I was wrong, huh?"

Frank peeled off his gloves and parka, which she took and hung up by the fire to dry.

"Let me light a few more lamps, then I need to start the generator." She walked to the table beside the front door and picked up the matches.

"I can go start the generator for you."

"You just came in from the cold. Besides, I'd have to do it myself if you weren't here."

"But I am here, so let me help. It's the least I can do since you opened your door to someone you thought would be a stranger." He donned his coat and gloves again and headed for the door. "Where exactly is the generator?" The flashlight he'd carried in was back in his hand as he waited by the front door for her directions.

"If you go through the kitchen and out the backdoor, then turn to your right, you'll see the shed. The genny is full of fuel and ready to go. Thanks, Frank."

Once he walked out the door, her previous thoughts of him came back to her.

What are the odds I'd think of him and he'd end up on my doorstep?

While she waited for Frank to return, she finished lighting the lamps in the living room and made sure the fire had enough wood to last a few hours.

CHAPTER TWO

"DAMN, it's cold out here." The wind took his breath the second he opened his mouth and spoke.

Sarah. My God, how did I not know she's living here? She's only about forty minutes from the lodge.

The wind increased and tried to blow him back as the all too eager drifting snow threatened to engulf him on his trek to the generator shed. A gust blew the shed door back against the wall when he opened it. He used both hands to jerk the door shut then swung the flashlight around to illuminate the machinery.

"Nice set up, top of the line equipment. At least she knows what she's doing up here in the middle of winter. She always was a smart girl."

The generator started with an easy flip of a switch.

A smile grew on his face while he reminisced about Sarah as a teen.

"God, I was stupid back then." If only he'd have paid attention and spoke his mind. Things might be so different now. Sarah could have been his and he wouldn't have had to keep up with her through her brother. The wind stole the self-deprecating chuckle that burst out of him when he stepped out of the shed and headed for the house. If only he'd been brave enough to tell her how he felt about her and less worried about how Alan would react to finding out his best friend was in love with his little sister.

Thankfully, the shed wasn't far from the house. The snow didn't seem to have any inclination of stopping soon and the temperature seemed to have dropped twenty degrees since he arrived. This was going to be a long night, not that he minded being with Sarah, but he had a business to get back to and guests to check on. They were booked to capacity, and the skiing had been excellent. Maybe Sarah would agree to go back with him, so he could treat her to dinner as a thank you for taking him in.

He shook off the snow clinging to him before carefully opening the back door. "The genny's running. Man, is it cold out there."

Sarah was standing there with her hand out. "Thank you, now give me your coat."

He removed his coat and watched snow melt and drip off as he handed it to Sarah.

"Get those boots off and set them by the fire. I'll make some coffee, or would you prefer some chai tea?" The lamp she carried lit up the kitchen nicely when she took his coat and hung it up in the utility room off the kitchen.

He unlaced his boots, pulled them off, and placed them by the fire and returned to the kitchen. "Coffee and I don't agree this late unless I'm behind on work. Chai tea sounds perfect. I suppose there's no cell service available at the moment."

"Nope. I checked while you were braving the storm, again, to start the genny. Sorry." She placed a mug in the sink and filled the teakettle, then set it on the stove and lit the burner with a long match. "Water won't take too long to heat up."

He slid a chair out and sat down at the table. Her smile still warmed his heart. "So what made you move out here?" And just as quickly her bright smile disappeared. *Brilliant, you know her husband died. That has to be part of the reason she moved.*

"My husband passed away after an accident. This was our vacation home. I couldn't bring myself to part with it. Plus, this is the perfect place for me to write and enjoy some solitude after the rush of L.A." She turned her back to him and grabbed a couple mugs from the cupboard.

"I'm sorry. Alan told me about your husband's accident. I should have known."

"Why would you? It's not like we all spent vacations here together. There's no reason you'd know about this place." A slight smile reappeared on her face when she rested her hand on his shoulder and gave him a reassuring squeeze.

"So, any plans for the holidays?"

"Not really. Nice change of subject." The teakettle whistled and she set about making their tea.

The smile returned to her face and warmed up the room.

Now to find out why she doesn't have anything planned for Christmas. She has a son, why isn't she spending the day with him?

A mug clinked down on the table in front of him, pulling him from his thoughts. "Thank you."

"Sure, let's move in by the fireplace where it's more comfortable." She led him into the living room and sat on the sofa.

"So what has you out in this nasty weather? Don't tell me you're on vacation at the lodge." She sipped her tea while she gazed at him waiting for an answer.

"Actually I own the lodge but was out checking a couple of my other businesses and thought I could get back before the snow hit. Guess I didn't leave soon enough." He'd overcorrected and ended up in the ditch not far from her driveway. The snowplow would bury his SUV if the snow kept up all night. "It was strange though, the storm wasn't all that strong, then all of a sudden it was like a tornado of snow grew up from the road and engulfed my car. I've never seen anything like it before."

"I think the storm started sooner than the weather people anticipated. It was probably just a gust of wind that made it look that way. How long have you owned the lodge?" She twisted to face him and placed her elbow on the back of the couch, leaning her head on her hand.

"I bought it eight years ago. The place had been such a big part of our lives, when it came up for sale I couldn't resist. As you know, I took marketing and business management at university, so I knew what I needed to do to keep the place running. Thankfully, I made good money during my first job. Then I started my own company, which helped make more. Learning the ropes in retail also helped prepare me for running the lodge with the ski shop attached."

"Sounds like you've done well for yourself. I'm impressed, but I always knew you'd do well. So what are the other businesses you were checking on, if you don't mind me asking?"

"I own a cattle ranch, and I'm a partner in a group that owns the mall in town." Her eyes still sparkled when she was curious about something. *At least some things never change.*

"What are you grinning about? I'm beginning to feel like the awkward teen I used to be when we were kids." She squirmed in her seat.

"Your eyes still twinkle when your curiosity is piqued."

She laughed aloud as a blush bloomed in her cheeks. "We had some good times back then, didn't we?"

"We sure did. How we stayed out of trouble is beyond me. Not to shift gears too fast, but don't you have a son?" The good vibes in the air dropped away again as her smile disappeared.

"Yes, he lives in Denver."

She visibly closed herself off. Something happened between mother and son, but what? With the loss of their husband and father, he expected them to be closer than most.

"I'm sorry. I didn't mean to open old wounds." He grasped her wrist and gave her a gentle squeeze.

She sat up and laid her hand over his on her arm. "I'm dealing in my own way."

The sad smile she sent his way plucked those all too

familiar heartstrings that seemed to connect him to her as if no time had passed. "Do you want to talk about it? Maybe I can help."

"Thank you, but there isn't much anyone can do. He won't see me or talk to me. He even returns my letters unopened. I used to leave messages on his answering machine but he never returned my calls, and the last time I tried to call I got the recording 'this number is no longer in service.'"

She tried to hide her tears, but the fire reflected off the wet trails left behind on her cheeks. "I guess it won't hurt, much, to tell you what happened. It's not like you're a stranger." She got up, sat on the floor, and poked at the fire. "Rick died because I made the decision to turn off the machines. Chris has never forgiven me for it."

"From what Alan told me, he wouldn't have recovered from his injuries. Is that true?"

"Yes. His brain had ceased to function. He was brain dead."

As she stared into the fire, he rose and moved to her.

"Then you had no choice. Didn't anyone explain this to your son?" He palmed her cheek and gently turned her face toward him.

Her son needed a healthy dose of reality. At fifteen, he was allowed a few stupid ideas. At twenty, he should know better and be making amends for being a complete ass the last few years.

"His grandparents tried several times, but he refused to listen to them too."

He leaned toward her and wiped a fresh tear from her cheek with his thumb. "You don't deserve to be treated this way. Someone needs to set that kid straight."

"I have faith he'll come around eventually. I continue to write my letters, and his grandparents still try to get through to him. We'll wear him down eventually." Her broken laugh tore at his heart.

"Well, if I can ever do anything for you, just say the word." He patted her arm and stood. He was suddenly antsy with nothing to do to work it out.

* * *

"FRANK—" Watching him stand and move closer to the fireplace, she almost called him back. What did he mean by his vague offer of assistance?

"Yes?" He stared into the fire and jabbed at the logs with the iron poker.

"Why did we stop talking when you went away to college? We lost so much time and a great friendship." Her stomach fluttered as she waited for his answer. *Why am I so nervous now, I wasn't when he sat here touching me?* She didn't want to think he didn't consider her a good enough friend to keep in contact with.

"Do you want the truth or an excuse?" He twisted around on his heels and met her gaze.

"The truth, please."

"I was an idiot. I went to college and played at being the big man on campus. Then once Alan told me you were getting married, I realized what I'd lost thinking I was more important than I was. After that, I stayed away and threw myself into business to forget. Met my late wife and moved on. You were never far from my thoughts, but I chose a different path and had no right to disrupt your life."

"I'm sorry for your loss, Frank. I can certainly empathize with you." The 'realized what I'd lost' comment wasn't *lost* on her. "What did you mean by 'realized what I'd lost'?"

"Nothing, it's history now anyway."

"Please tell me, Frank. I know you lost a chance at a new friendship. I think you and Rick would have been good friends." She tried to interpret the look on his face but the firelight kept the shadows dancing too much to see enough of his expression.

"You don't understand, I didn't want to like him. Never mind, I shouldn't have said that."

The fire popped and Frank turned back, pulling the screen shut on the fireplace. "What ifs will drive you crazy if you let them."

"No sense in wondering what if, Frank. Everything happens for a reason, even heartache. We wouldn't be the people we are without our pasts and the people we've met and loved along the way." His eyes glittered with the fire's dancing light when he looked at her, ending her impromptu words of wisdom.

"When did you become so philosophical, Miss Romantic?" His smile turned into a mischievous grin as he rose and offered her his hand.

"What are you thinking?" Hesitant, she slid her hand into his, ready to pull back should he try anything silly. The only thing he did was clasp her fingers and send a zing of electricity snapping across her skin.

"I think we need something to help pass the time besides digging up history." He pulled her close enough they were cheek to cheek and sang softly in her ear. He pulled the hand he held to his chest and wrapped his other arm around her waist, gently hugging her to him.

"You still have a great voice." He sounded the same as he did during their last family vacation together at the lodge when he did this very thing then as well. A warm puff of air tickled her neck, and she laughed lightly. "This is nice. Almost like old times."

Frank continued to sing and slow dance her around the cabin's small living room. The heat his body gave off seeped into her, helping her relax and enjoy the moment.

A girl could get used to this. Rick popped into her mind,

and guilt swept through her. Why was his memory intruding now? He hadn't invaded her thoughts as much in the past six months as he did in the past couple of days. *How odd.*

Frank stopped singing. "What's wrong?"

"Nothing."

He leaned back and looked her in the eyes. "Something happened, you suddenly turned into a statue."

"It's nothing, really. Just had a memory hit me from out of left field. Sorry." She pulled her hand from his grasp and stepped back out of his arms.

Nodding, he let her go. "I know how it feels. I've had a few memories sucker-punch me over the years."

"It's late, we might as well get some rest. It's possible we'll be holed up here for a few days before the plows get out this way. With the generator running, the furnace should keep it nice and warm, but if you get cold, there is a small wood-burning stove in the bedroom. There's enough wood in the woodbin beside it to last the night." He followed her to the door of the guestroom.

"With the equipment you have set up out there, I don't have any worries about the furnace not running through the night."

He stepped through the doorway into the bedroom, turned back to face her, and grabbed her hand. "Thank you for opening your door to me."

The warmth of his hand kissed her palm. "Goodnight, Frank."

She released his hand and made her way to her room.

A frustrated sigh slipped from her lips as she latched her bedroom door. "What is going on?" Rick continued to invade her thoughts, and now Frank slept in the extra bedroom, snowed in with her for the time being. He only lived about forty-five minutes up the road. She hoped now that he knew she lived here, she'd see more of him.

Is all this a coincidence or is something else going on? Is there such a thing as fate or destiny?

Frank's image appeared in her mind. He'd filled out and developed a healthy set of muscles. His toned body showed the proof he took advantage of the ski slopes.

Being in his arms made her aware of herself as a woman again. Could she handle the emotional baggage again? Did she want to? Being alone let her lose herself in her writing and taking care of the cabin. Now she thought about everything she'd left behind. Being a woman was complicated, and honestly, a pain in the ass.

Once she'd removed some of her warm layers, she climbed into bed. Thoughts of Frank rushed through her mind, ratcheting up her desire and raising her body heat. The sheets were cool, soothing her flushed skin.

Most of the night she tossed and turned, wondering about possibilities. Finally, her eyelids slid shut even though she fought against it.

* * *

A man's angry mutterings echoed through the mist as bright rays of light pierced through. In the distance the mist dissipated, revealing a pond on a warm summer day. The fog at her feet parted before her as she strolled closer to the water and spotted a lone figure throwing their arms out as if yelling at themselves.

"Damn it, way to go, idiot. You've screwed up again." Rick paced back and forth at the pond's edge.

Laughter bubbled up and erupted from her. "Rick? Is everything okay?"

"Hello, love. Sorry I ruined such a nice time with Frank. I don't think I'm ever going to get the hang of communicating with you when you're awake." He looked contrite.

The breath caught in her throat. "That was you earlier?"

"I wanted you to remember more about Frank but didn't have the

energy to do anything but make you remember me." His brow was pinched just like it always was when he was frustrated and concentrating on something.

"Do you truly want me to move on?" She wished she could touch him just once and be able to feel it. Dreams weren't created that way though.

"Yes, you deserve more happiness in your life. You need to stop hiding from the world and live again. There's too much out there for you to shut yourself up in this cabin."

Isolating herself had been her way of protecting herself from feeling. Even Christopher's hatred was easier to handle when she didn't have to face happy parents with their kids on a daily basis.

"Why aren't you grabbing this opportunity? I remember Frank, and I know what you felt for him, even though you thought otherwise. Christmas is fast approaching, time to give yourself a new start."

"But I can't. I can't risk my heart again."

"We will always love one another, but you have so much life yet to live and love to give. Grab it and take the chance. You'll never know if you don't try. Don't hesitate too long, you'll miss out on so much."

"How can you stand there and tell me to love someone else?"

"It's easy, like I said before, I love you enough to want to see you happy…love again, Sarah…." With those last words, he faded away and the mist engulfed the landscape until everything went dark.

* * *

LIGHT filtered through the curtains, hitting her in the face.

"Morning already? It feels like I just fell asleep. Ugh!" Rolling to her back, she stared at the ceiling. The scent of waffles and sausage reached her nose. "Frank." How could she forget Frank slept in the guestroom last night?

"Waffles?" She didn't have readymade waffles in the house. "He can cook—from scratch?"

Sarah popped up and grabbed her sweats and bulky sweater. She finished her morning ritual of washing her face and brushing her teeth, dressed, and headed for the kitchen. A man cooking in her kitchen was something she needed to see to believe.

Mouthwatering scents wafted through the cabin. Waffles didn't normally interest her, but these smelled like heaven.

The sight at the stove stopped her in mid-stride. Tall, muscular, broad shoulders, tight butt, and just a sprinkling of gray around the edges of dark mahogany hair, Frank had grown into a very handsome man and seeing him cooking breakfast was wonderful first thing in the morning. *Thank God for gas stoves.* A soft chuckle escaped her, but the sound registered enough for him to hear.

A sparkling smile and twinkling brown eyes greeted her. "Perfect timing, I was just about to come get you. Breakfast is ready."

"I smelled waffles. I can't believe you made them from scratch."

"I hope you don't mind, but I found some blueberries in your freezer and added some to the warm syrup." His expectant gaze met hers over the cooking food, appearing to judge her reaction.

"That's perfect, I love fruit in my syrup. I do the same for my pancakes, if I don't put the fruit directly in the batter." She opened the china cabinet and pulled out two plates along with a small syrup boat.

"Good idea. It'll be a lot easier to pour the syrup from the boat instead of the saucepan. I'm not the neatest person in the world. I can use all the help I can get." Frank carried the platter of waffles and sausage links to the table and took the syrup boat back with him. After placing the boat in the sink, he poured the warm syrup and fruit into the container, and then grabbed silverware for the two of them on his way back to the table.

"This is wonderful, Frank. Thank you." The waffles were fluffy when she speared a couple with the serving fork. "Wow, where did you learn how to make them so light and fluffy?"

"If you think these are great, I'll have to make you my chocolate dessert waffles some time. I got the recipes from my wife's mother. She was a lovely woman and a terrific cook." Frank filled his plate as he talked.

"You really loved her." She loved Rick's parents and could understand if his ex-mother-in-law was as terrific as Rick's mother.

"I did, she passed away a year before my wife. Which I'm happy for, it would have destroyed her to watch Janet waste away from the cancer."

The sad turn of the conversation had her contemplating the turn her life had taken as well. So into her own thoughts, she didn't notice he'd become quiet until she finished the food on her plate.

"Sorry, I didn't mean to bring up painful memories again. Breakfast was a nice surprise. Thank you." She cleared the table and took everything to the sink. "Go in and relax, I'll clean up and be with you shortly."

"There's no reason I can't help. It's not like I can go anywhere and my to-do list is extremely short. I already did the walkway, so that's off the list. Next, drying dishes." He flashed a half-smile and shrugged.

"You shoveled this morning too? You didn't have to do that. As soon as Mr. Jones gets his place cleared, he'll be here to clear the driveway." She shook her head and smiled. "You're doing too much."

"I wasn't doing anything else. The workout did me good." He grabbed the towel and began drying the dishes as she set them in the drainer.

They spent the remainder of the day catching up on each other's lives and trading vacation stories.

After dinner they sat on the sofa finishing their earlier conversation.

"Janet used to love to sit on the beach." A faraway look entered his eyes.

What type of woman had Janet been to catch his heart? "Tell me about her." She covered his hand with hers and gave a gentle squeeze as he stared into the fire.

"You'd have loved her. She loved life and laughing was her favorite thing to do. We met when I bowled her over in the hallway about two years into my first job after college. It was on from there."

The sparkle came back to his eyes as he talked about his late wife.

"She must have been a special woman to catch your attention." She smiled at him before turning to stare at the fire.

"She was. My dad always said she carried an 'old soul.' She possessed wisdom beyond her years and always seemed to know things without any logical explanation. Actually, Janet reminded me of you in many ways." He turned his hand over under hers and entwined their fingers. "Thank you for asking about her. It feels good to talk about her with someone."

"I've enjoyed listening to you talk about her. I wish I could have met her. It's been nice to talk about Rick, too, especially with someone who understands." Tucking her feet up under her, she leaned into Frank and laid her head on his shoulder. Reliving old memories with Frank led her into familiar territory, reminding her of the old days.

Her heart ached as the sensation of someone palming the back of her head sent a calming wave through her.

Thank you, Rick.

CHAPTER THREE

JERKING awake to the heavy thumping of Rob Zombie, the room spun before her mind settle, and she realized the radio alarm was going off. The electric company finally restored the power. *The phone will be working now too.* Frank would leave as soon as the roads were cleared and someone got out there to retrieve his vehicle.

Burrowing down into the blankets, she hoped to hold off the day. He had to get back to the lodge and work, but she wasn't ready for their time to be over or to be alone again. She'd grown used to having him around in the short time the storm had stranded him with her.

A knock on her bedroom door pulled her from her thoughts, making her sit up and grudgingly get out of bed. "Just a minute, please."

"No problem, I just wanted to let you know the phones are working and I reached the lodge. Everything is fine and the staff who were stuck there have kept the guests occupied. The roads are still impassable though, so you're stuck with me for a little longer."

She heard his quiet chuckle through the door.

"I'm having fun being *stuck* with you. Being able to catch up with your life has been great. I'm glad the storm happened when it did. Who knows how long we would have gone on not knowing we lived so close to each other."

After her morning ritual and pulling on her yoga pants, thick socks, and favorite sweater, she opened the door to see Frank's smiling face. "Good morning."

"Good morning to you too, pretty lady. Any requests for

breakfast?" He leaned on her doorframe while he waited for her answer.

"Oh no, it's my turn to cook for you. Do you like asparagus? I make great asparagus and goat cheese omelets." Once in the kitchen and with her head stuck in the refrigerator, she added, "The goat cheese is a bit tangy if you aren't familiar with it. I use a garlic and herb goat cheese, it adds great flavor to the omelet."

"I like asparagus, but I'll have to take your word on the goat cheese."

He chuckled as she pulled the eggs and a small pack of bacon from the fridge. "How do you have asparagus though? That isn't quite in season around here."

"I freeze and can it when I can find nice spears cheap enough to buy in large quantities."

She cracked three eggs into a bowl, grabbed a whisk, and scrambled them. She then handed Frank the jar of asparagus to open.

"You certainly have turned into quite the homemaker, haven't you? Canning?"

The dumbfounded look on his face amused her. She raised a brow at him while slicing a few asparagus spears, and then dumped everything into the skillet.

"Don't look so surprised. I'm not completely useless." Watching his mouth fall open and his complexion pale a shade or two, she hid the smile that threatened to give her away.

"Sarah, I've never once imagined you as useless." His hand shot out to grip her arm, stopping her as she passed by on the way to the fridge.

She laughed outright this time and fought to get it under control. Once she had a handle on it, she took a breath. "Still easy. I'm just teasing you. You fell for it, like you used to." She patted his cheek while she pulled from his grasp and took the cheese from the fridge. "Will you flip the bacon, please?"

"Sure. That's a small package of cheese. How do you use it?" He moved in close as she opened the goat cheese log and crumbled it with a fork before dropping the bits onto the egg and asparagus mixture in the pan.

"That's how. I can't wait to find out what you think." She folded the cooked egg mixture and slid the finished omelet onto a plate with a few slices of bacon. "Now for mine." She prepared her eggs and asparagus. As she added the cheese she looked up to see him not eating. "Don't wait for me, eat while the food is warm."

His eyelids slid shut as he slowly chewed the first bite of omelet.

Frank's eyes opened slowly, and he stood. He looked as if he had won some great prize as he came around the table and stopped just inches from her. His palms were warm on her cheeks as he held her face and kissed her soundly on the lips. "This is the best omelet I've ever eaten. You have to give my chef at the lodge the recipe."

"Um…okay." She pulled back. Once the shock from his spontaneous kiss wore off, heat rushed into her cheeks. The air around her cooled as he stepped back, looking a bit embarrassed. Calming her pounding heart, the food about to burn on the stove suddenly became very interesting.

* * *

THE plows barreled down the road for the third time, leaving yet another drift at the end of her driveway. Thankfully, Mr. Jones was there clearing the mounds of snow, and of course, Frank was out there helping.

The day was passing too quickly for her liking. She refilled thermoses with hot coffee and delivered them to a very thankful Mr. Jones and Frank. She should be happy things were getting back to normal. The sooner Frank returned to his life, the sooner she could get on with hers. Her deadline loomed and she hadn't written a single word in the fifty-four hours and forty-eight minutes they were snowed in together. It was time to settle down and write.

Ideas were swarming, so her daily word count goal wouldn't be hard to reach. Reality was about to hit her leading couple, and she couldn't wait to get started.

"Hey, Sarah, we're done!" Frank kicked off his boots and carried in an arm load of wood for the fire. "Mr. Jones said thanks for the coffee and if you need him for anything you're supposed to call him. He's a very nice old man. I can't believe how energetic he is. Hell, he was raring to go plow some more snow, and I'm ready for a nap." The corners of his eyes crinkled when he laughed, his jovial tone brightened the room.

"He's been a great friend and a big help since I moved here permanently. He comes over in the spring to till up the garden for me as well." Her writing called to her. The leading couple was ready to get the show on the road.

"Earth to Sarah."

She nearly jumped out of her skin when a hand gripped her forearm.

"Sorry, Frank, what did you say?"

"Where did you go?" The look of concern on his face warmed another small piece of her heart.

"I was just thinking about my writing. I haven't done any since the storm hit."

"I almost forgot you're a big shot author now. So what do you write? Let me guess, romance, right?"

"Ha, ha, smart aleck. No, I do not write romance. I write mysteries. Ever heard of M.C. Gibbs?" She headed for the living room and the bookshelf behind the sofa.

He stayed right on her heels. "Oh my God, you can't be serious. *No One's Child*, right? That was Janet's favorite book. She even made me sit and listen as she read aloud to me. I have to say the story is brilliant." He acted as though he'd reverted to an eight-year-old boy, his excitement evident in his voice.

Her face heated as his praise caught her off guard. She never dreamed he'd know her work. "Thank you. I'm glad the two of you enjoyed it."

"Enjoyed it? Janet loved all your books. I wish I'd known you were the author. It would have made her day to have met the woman behind the stories." He laid his arm over her shoulders as he looked at the shelf of books she'd penned.

"Meeting a fan would have been wonderful for me too. As you can probably guess, I don't meet many." She turned and pulled several of her books off the shelf and handed them to him. "Here, have you read these?"

"No, I haven't. Normally I don't have much downtime. But I'll make the time now that I know the author." He winked as he took the books from her.

As he grasped the books, his fingers grazed hers. She almost pulled away but looked him in the eye, losing herself in his gaze. The books made a dull thud as they hit the sofa cushion just before he leaned in and palmed her cheek. Her heart raced as his lips drew closer and closer. *Kiss me already!*

She took the initiative and went up on tiptoe, pressing her mouth to his. His lips were softer than she anticipated. The modest kiss in the kitchen at breakfast wasn't even a clue as to what a real kiss from him would be like. *Lord, he's talented.* His tongue traced the seam of her lips and she parted them, allowing him entrance. He worshipped her mouth as he deepened the kiss, stealing her breath.

Heavy pounding on the front door brought her plummeting back to Earth.

"Sorry, Sarah. I shouldn't have done that. I was out of line." Remorse flashed in his eyes, but his actions didn't show one ounce of regret. If anything his licking his lips and his gaze barely leaving her mouth screamed he'd kiss her again given the chance. He'd have a chance if she had anything to do with it. *Wow!*

"You have no reason to apologize. I enjoyed our first kiss." She winked in hopes of lightening the slightly uncomfortable situation.

Knock, knock, knock.

"Guess the roads are finally open. But I'm not expecting anyone." She backed out of his embrace and headed for the door.

"It's probably Tom from the lodge. He said he'd get here as soon as he finished clearing the parking lot." The heat from his hand warmed her flesh where his palm rested on her hip, stopping her from continuing to the door. "Let me treat you to a fabulous dinner at the lodge this Friday as a thank you for taking me in."

She turned in his arms, and he rested his forehead against hers.

"Oh, I suppose I can tolerate your company for a little longer."

"Good because I'm not ready to lose the connection we're rebuilding."

Bam, bam, bam.

"Damn, whoever is beating on my door sure is persistent."

Frank laughed as he released his hold on her and answered the door.

"Hi, Tom, come in out of the cold. I'd like you to meet someone." Frank moved back and let the older man enter the cabin. "Tom, this is Sarah, a great blast from my past. Sarah, this is Tom. I couldn't keep the lodge going without him."

"*Pfft*, right." The older man took his hat off, and he wasn't much older than Frank. His obviously premature gray hair belied the youthful glow in his eyes and face. He offered her his hand. "Hello, ma'am, nice to meet you."

"Please, call me Sarah, and nice to meet you too." She

appreciated that he didn't hold her hand like it might shatter if he closed his fingers the slightest bit. She couldn't stand a limp handshake.

"Sarah will be joining us for dinner at the lodge Friday night at seven, Tom." The warm weight of Frank's arm rested across her shoulders as he smiled and pulled her closer.

"That's great. Hope you enjoy the lodge and the food. Our chef is amazing." Tom nodded, and looked at Frank. "Are you ready? There are some things you need to take care of before your date."

Sarah glanced up at him, and then at Frank and frowned. "Since when is it a date?"

"Just humor him, he's teasing." Frank slapped Tom on the shoulder and pushed him toward the door. Turning back to Sarah, he whispered, "Would it be so bad if it was a date?" He winked as heat bloomed in her cheeks. "Anyone ever tell you, you're cute when you blush?"

* * *

FRANK walked out and pulled the door shut before she formulated a response. "I want to send the limo for her if the roads are clear enough. She deserves the best I can give her."

"Sure, the roads seem in decent shape right now. If not we can equip the Hummer with the same amenities to pick her up." Tom squeezed his shoulder. "She's someone pretty special, isn't she?"

"Yes, she's extremely special." A grin spread across his face. Sarah had always been special. He'd let her slip from his life once, he wasn't going to let her disappear again, not without doing everything within his power to keep her close.

Easy conversation filled the ride back to the lodge. Tom relayed everything that happened while he sat stranded and enjoying himself at Sarah's house. "Enjoying myself…I wish. Don't get me wrong, seeing her again and catching up on her life was great, but I'm kicking myself for holding back all this time. I should have at least told her how I felt, how I still feel about her."

"You couldn't be anything less than a perfect gentleman, and we both know it. She doesn't seem to be in any rush to be rid of you. I think you have time to tell her. Besides, she seems confident enough in herself, she'd have pushed you away if you'd pushed her toward something she wasn't ready for."

Tom knew him too well and seemed to have an instant understanding of Sarah.

"How do you know people with just an introduction?" Frank studied the man beside him, the man he'd known for most of his adult life.

"My mother always told me to trust my intuition. I've followed her advice and never been wrong, to my knowledge." His light laughter broke up the seriousness of the conversation.

"To your knowledge, huh?" He doubted Tom had ever been wrong about someone in his life. "You have her pegged though. She'd have kicked my behind if I'd pushed her."

When they pulled into the lodge, Tom dropped him off at the door to the ski shop. "I'll catch up with you later to confirm the time for Sarah's pick-up on Friday. Thanks for everything, Tom." He turned to head inside but stopped short. "Hey, Tom, before you go, will you do me a favor and see if you can find a current phone number for this guy?" He grabbed a clipboard from between the seats and wrote down the information Tom needed to run a quick search.

"Sure, I can do it as soon as I get the truck put away. I'll come find you when I have what you need."

"Thanks for everything, man." He shook hands with Tom before he hurried into the building.

The ski shop was quiet and neat. At least he could trust the team he'd put together to help him run the lodge during the busiest seasons. He moved through the lodge and entered the kitchen.

"Jacob, I need you to come up with a brilliant dinner for two Friday night at seven."

His chef was a master in the kitchen. He'd leave everything in Jacob's capable hands, knowing Sarah and he would have a great culinary experience.

"Sure, Frank. What do you have in mind? Or are you up for a surprise?"

"I trust you to know what to serve. Surprise us."

Jacob Vincent had thirty years of experience and could cook anything anyone requested, as long as the ingredients were available. Frank made sure the lodge's kitchen came fully loaded with top-of-the-line equipment and kept the pantry fully stocked at all times. Even during the off-season, he lived there year-round and kept the hotel going in the summer, open for those who liked to hike and fish. Of course, the summer months weren't quite as lucrative as the winter months. More people visited for the skiing.

"I need to sweep her off her feet."

"Little quick, isn't it? You were only stranded with her for a few days." Jacob laughed and cocked an eyebrow at him.

He laughed at the chef. "She's a longtime friend who I'd like to make a permanent fixture in my life."

"Ah, I see. Well, I have the perfect main course in mind. I'll make sure I have what I need and get started on the rest of the menu." Chef Jacob shook his hand and turned toward the pantry.

He stopped the on-staff floral designer and sent her Frank's way before disappearing through the kitchen swinging doors.

"Mr. Taylor? Chef said you might need my assistance." A new addition to the lodge, Amy had proven her talent on numerous occasions. The floral arrangements at the lodge were beautiful and always a topic of conversation with the older female guests.

"Hello, Amy. Yes, I need a pretty bouquet made up for a special friend, if we have the flowers to spare." Frank couldn't remember the schedule for flower delivery without looking up the lodge's calendar on his computer. The food and liquor schedules were memorized, but the floral deliveries were a new addition.

"Sure thing. I just got off the phone with the florist. Our order will be here in a couple hours."

They discussed the size of bouquet, Sarah, and what flowers would be best to help convey his feelings for her. Once he'd sent Amy on her way, he entered his office and called housekeeping to set up a private table for their dinner in the small boardroom next door to his office. Now the rest of the evening was up to him.

"Hey, boss. I have that phone number you wanted." Tom walked into the office and gave him the information.

"You're a lifesaver, Tom. Thanks again for doing this for me." Now he could try and set things up for Christmas.

"You're welcome. Hope everything works out. I'll be heading home now. Call if you need me for anything." Tom waved as he left the office.

An hour later, he hung up the phone. He'd managed to stay calm and polite during the conversation. It was a tough call but one he needed to make, and hopefully his plans would all come together over Christmas, which was rapidly approaching. Not much time to get everything arranged, yet just enough for it all to blow up in his face. Mentally keeping his fingers crossed, he called Tom and told him go ahead and use the Hummer to pick up Sarah. The SUV was safer in the snow, not to mention roomier than the limo.

When he had the dinner and extras for the evening set up, he checked in with everyone, and called it an early night, retreating to the owner's suite. Dinner was going to be perfect. His capable staff would do their best. He'd thought about having dinner in his suite but didn't want her to think he had an ulterior motive. He'd take his time and woo Sarah, as he should have years ago. Woo? Where did that come from? His word choice made him laugh but quickly realized that was exactly what he needed to do to win her heart.

He needed to do everything possible to win her. She would know how he felt before their night was over, he'd make sure of it. Hope bloomed in his chest as he thought that he might actually pull their date and her Christmas present off without a hitch. Fate hadn't stranded him at her house for nothing.

CHAPTER FOUR

THE stars shined bright, their light blazing through her window as she lay staring at the ceiling, trying to go to sleep but failing miserably. Her date tomorrow night weighed heavily on her mind. "What am I doing? Do I really want to put myself out there again?"

Talking to herself didn't gain her any answers. Maybe if she tossed the questions out into the universe someone would find the answers for her before she drove herself crazy.

One word breathed across her face. *Relax....*

This was one of those moments she was glad she lived alone—no one to see her hearing voices and talking to her dead husband. "Rick?"

Silence greeted her at first.

*Let go...*whispered through the room.

"Oh my God, will you stop? You make things sound so simple and easy. Well, they're not easy or simple. Not for me." She reached out and grabbed her pen and notebook with the urge to write an argument between her hero and heroine.

An hour later with Rick and Frank forgotten, she fell into a fitful sleep.

* * *

STANDING in the shadow of the old oak, she watched as someone walked out the back door. Rick strode toward her.

"I'd forgotten how frustrating you can be. Why are you so nervous about your date? It's Frank, it's not like he's a stranger you're just getting to know. I know you have a few years to get caught up on, but you were off to a great start while he was snowed in with you."

He reached out to touch her, and she remembered the familiar feel of his hand brushing softly against her cheek.

She leaned into the sensation while a tear slipped down her face. "I miss you."

"I miss you, too, but you have so much more to do before we're together again. Have fun and spend it with someone you love. Frank loves you, he always has. I can see it, you have to see it too." He smiled and the colors of his shirt and pants began to lighten. He blurred around the edges.

"Why are you going already? You just got here."

"It's time to wake up and start your day. Remember to enjoy yourself this evening. Stop worrying and just have fun. Reenter the land of the living, Sarah…please…."

Rick's form became transparent and slowly faded from sight.

* * *

SUNLIGHT breached her eyelids even though she tried to avoid the rays, not ready to leave Rick. Their time together never lasted long enough. There was always more she wanted to say, but she could never remember everything when the dreams started. And they were over before she knew it.

Frank. Tonight she'd be having dinner with Frank at the lodge. Was he serious about it being a date? *What should I wear?*

She needed to do what Rick said, stop worrying and just live in the moment. Frank never mentioned wanting a relationship. Maybe she read more into what had been said than was actually there. After all, he'd spent almost three days with her and not said anything. He'd only given her a peck in the kitchen and kissed her once just before he left.

Wishful thinking, Sarah. Stop procrastinating and get on with the day. Rolling to her right, she tossed her legs over the side of the bed and sat up. Her favorite fuzzy slippers warmed her feet as she stood and moved across the room to the bathroom, another upgrade she'd added when she decided to live here permanently. There had only been one bathroom at the end of the hall. She hated having to wait, so she contacted a contractor to build an en suite off the master bedroom.

The woman looking back at her seemed to be aging gracefully. Only a few small age spots here and there, along with some tiny lines around her eyes and mouth revealed her age to be more than she liked. "Not bad. Could be worse, I suppose."

Thank God her coffeemaker had a timer. She needed a mug of liquid energy before she crawled back into bed and begged out of Frank's dinner invitation. She might even need some liquid courage before dinner tonight, depending on how the morning shaped up.

What made her so nervous about dinner? Her hesitancy would make sense if Frank were a stranger, but he wasn't, she'd known him most of her life. Were the emotions of her teenage crush fueling her case of nerves? Had she been transported to those angst-filled days of longing for him and never getting him, or was her past stirring up old feelings of inadequacy?

"For Pete's sake, I'm an adult, not some teenage girl unsure of herself." She'd go have dinner and a nice evening with Frank, and that would put an end to this tension. He was always the gentleman and obviously wanted to rekindle their friendship. If he had wanted more from her, he would have shown some sign while they were stranded together the past three days. Wouldn't he?

Once she'd convinced herself dinner would just be dinner, she got on with her day as usual. Breakfast went down easier and she even managed to get some writing done. Not enough to complete the book but at least she'd gotten something down. She'd take the small accomplishments as they came. Her life had stalled over the past several months so she counted every little thing she completed, even the smallest amount of writing. Looking at the word count, she was surprised to see she'd written more than she thought, which made her look at the clock.

Shit! Terrific, now I'll be late.

With her household chores done and the wood hurriedly restocked, she headed for the shower. The warm water flowed over her as she wondered what to wear. Nerves screamed back in the minute she realized she'd no idea what he'd planned. So without knowing any details she didn't know what to wear.

She shut off the water, climbed from the shower, and grabbed her robe from the hook on the door. "Okay, Sarah, don't drive yourself crazy. You're only going to the lodge. A sweater and nice slacks will be fine." Her favorite oatmeal colored sweater with the cowl neck would be a perfect fit with her chocolate brown dress pants. Her brown high-heeled boots would complete the outfit.

Could she still use a curling iron? She hadn't bothered with one in years. *Might as well give it a shot and at least make an effort to look decent.* She plugged in the iron, and then started in on her makeup.

"You're too old for this stuff, ya know?" But it sure felt good to have a reason to dress up and look her best, even if the occasion was just dinner with an old friend. She smiled at the pretty woman looking back at her from the mirror. "You clean up pretty well for an old lady." She laughed as she unplugged the curling iron and put the makeup back in the case.

The boots she wanted were in the back of her closet. Once she'd crawled halfway in, someone knocked on her door. "Ugh! Figures he'd show up now." She laughed at her predicament and stood.

She was still laughing when she opened the door and saw Frank there with a bouquet of deep-red roses and bright-white baby's breath. "Oh, Frank, they are beautiful. Come in while I put on my boots." She admired his freshly shaven face, crisp, clean cologne, and then took the flowers from him. "Let me put these in some water and I'll be right with you."

Looking down at her stocking-feet, he chuckled. "Why don't you tell me where the vase is, I'll put them in water and you can finish what you were doing." He flashed her his brilliant smile and took the flowers back. As he did so, his fingers brushed hers, and a tingle rushed up her arm.

Keeping control of her reaction, she managed to pull back slowly, and direct him to the kitchen. "Thank you, Frank. The vases are in the small cupboard above the refrigerator." She went back to her room, retrieved the boots from the closet, and slid her feet into them.

Frank met her back in the living room carrying the vase of flowers and set them on the mantel. She'd move them when she returned so she'd be able to start a fire in the fireplace. Hopefully curling up on the couch with a hot cup of tea in front of a roaring fire would be the perfect end to a perfect dinner date.

Frank helped her on with her coat, his hands settling comfortably on her shoulders. "Ready?"

When she nodded, he opened the door and offered his arm. He tucked her hand into the crook of his elbow, and the warmth of his touch reached more than the cool flesh of her hand. A black Hummer sat in her driveway. As they approached, Tom appeared out of nowhere to hold the rear door open for them.

"Good evening, Ms. Wilson. I'll be your driver and hope you enjoy the night's festivities." Tom bit down on his lips, obviously trying hard not to laugh at his attempt at formality.

"Thank you, kind sir. I'm sure I will." She winked and earned a lighthearted laugh from their makeshift chauffer.

"Very funny, Tom." Frank handed her into the back of the Hummer. "Let's get going. I can't wait to see what she thinks of dinner."

"I'm right here, ya know?" She couldn't help but laugh as a blush crept up Frank's neck.

"Sorry, was just telling Tom to get a move on." He climbed in beside her before Tom closed the door and got behind the wheel. "Can I get you something to drink?"

Glancing around, the bar on the right side of the vehicle caught her eye. "Well, what do you have in stock?"

"I have everything for a mojito, if you still enjoy those." He flashed her a knowing grin, waiting for her answer.

"Oh my God, I can't believe you remember. I got in so much trouble back then." The skin of her face heated with the memory of her sixteenth birthday. She'd gotten drunk on mojitos without her parents finding out until her brother accidentally ratted her out the next day when he teased her about her hangover.

"Yeah, your parents called mine to see if I knew anything about it. I caught hell about that night too." His laugh made her heart happy. "I still can't figure out how you got those drinks without getting busted."

"Honestly, I can't remember how I did it. But to answer your question, yes, I still enjoy mojitos and would love one." He'd surprised her with the stretch Hummer and stocked bar, and impressed her with his idea of a date so far.

He handed her the drink and turned back to get one for himself.

"This is really good. You've obviously practiced mixing drinks." She sipped the minty drink and reminded herself to go slow. Too much alcohol on an empty stomach was not a good idea.

"Oh, I've definitely had practice. Needed the skill when I first opened the lodge with only a skeleton crew. I've worn multiple hats since college." He chuckled as he sat back down beside her to sip his scotch.

She sat in silence as they continued to the lodge, but Frank fidgeted next to her. *What is going on with him?*

"Frank, I appreciate the flowers and the Hummer ride, but what's going on?" She struggled to keep a blank expression on her face, not allowing the sudden pessimism to show through.

He reached out and grasped her free hand. "You deserve the best, and I plan to give you what I can. It's the least I can do after you opened your home to me. And didn't mace me when you opened the door." He winked mischievously.

Her surprise must have shown on her face.

He laughed. "What? You didn't think I noticed you slip the small canister into the drawer in the hall table, did you?"

She smiled up at him as her cheeks tingled with embarrassment. "No, I thought I'd been smooth and kept it out of sight. Sorry, a girl can't be too careful these days."

He leaned in and kissed the side of her head. "I'm glad you pay attention to your surroundings and take precautions for your safety."

"You didn't have to do all this just to say thank you. I was glad to have the chance to catch up with you. We drifted apart and missed out on a lot in each other's lives."

He slid closer and put his arm over her shoulders, pulling her snug against his side. "Yes, we did, but we've been given the chance to make up for some of the missed time now. I plan on taking advantage and enjoying your company as much as you'll allow me."

A comfortable silence filled the rest of their drive, as she sat with her head resting on his shoulder and his arm around her. It didn't matter what he'd planned, she'd enjoy their evening together and deal with anything else as it came.

The Hummer slowed and turned into the driveway leading to the lodge. "We're here. I can't wait to see what Jacob, our chef, has created for dinner. I left the meal up to him. He's very good at his job."

She chuckled at Frank's childish exuberance. His happiness

at the small things lightened her heart.

Tom pulled up in front of the lodge and let them out. "Hope you have a wonderful evening, Sarah."

"Thank you, Tom. I'm sure I will." She looked up at the facade of the large log structure. "The main building is just as I remember. Beautiful."

"I did a lot of work on the place, but wanted to keep the original facade the same. Wait till you see the inside." Once again, the joy showed through on his face. Frank was very proud of the lodge. And from what she had seen so far, he had every right to be.

He laid a protective hand on the small of her back as he walked her up the steps to the front doors. Stopping long enough to open the door for her, he then led her into the lodge. "Let's stop in my office and lose these coats." Hanging his coat on the coat rack, he turned to her as she shrugged out of hers. He caught her parka and hung it next to his. "Let me show you around. We've done a lot of updating and remodeling. I'd love to know what you think of the improvements."

The large rock fireplace and vaulted ceilings still graced the main room. Frank had updated the lighting fixtures and painstakingly stripped the dark wood paneling back to its natural lighter color.

"You changed the panoramic window. The floor to ceiling view is beautiful. You can see so much more. Great choice." She loved how the window followed the line of the ceiling, giving an uninterrupted view of the gorgeous snowy vista before them.

While showing her around the rest of the lodge he described the newly remodeled guest rooms. "The rooms hadn't changed much from when we used to come here. I updated the décor and made them more luxurious with thicker, richer fabrics and carpeting. And here we are, back where we started. We can sit and chat while we wait for dinner to be served."

The office was a warm and inviting room, with a large walnut desk and matching leather desk chair. The bookshelves behind the desk impressed her more. Floor to ceiling and not a bare spot to be found. There were books stacked on top of each other. "Um, don't you think it might be time to expand the shelves or reduce the number of books you have on these?"

Warm hands came to rest on her shoulders. "No, I just need to take the overflow back upstairs to my place."

She closed her eyes for a moment while she soaked in the body heat radiating from him. "You live upstairs? I remember you said you lived here, but I thought you meant in one of the personal chalets on the property."

"I thought about rehabbing one, but we decided the chalets rented too well to take one off the schedule. When I went up to check the third floor, I realized the space was perfect for what I needed. Plus, I could work on one room at a time and still be here to manage the lodge." Pride swelled in his voice as he told her what else he'd done to the interior of the lodge over the last few years.

The phone rang and interrupted his tale of updating the kitchen and expanding the dining room. "Excuse me for a moment." He stepped away and picked up the receiver. "Hello...yes. Thanks, Jacob, we'll be right there."

While he spoke on the phone, she took a closer look at the books on the shelves. Several murder mysteries caught her eye, along with her books, which were well worn. Someone had read these copies well and often. Her heart swelled knowing they were liked enough to be read more than once.

"Sarah, that was the chef. Our dinner is ready." He held his hand out to her.

"I can't wait to see what he's created for us." Taking his

offered hand, she let him lead her to where they were to have dinner. "All your raving has wet my appetite."

When Frank swung the door next to his office open, the flowers and table setting took her breath. Roses and calla lilies filled the perimeter of the room while a trio of white pillar candles with a deep red tablecloth adorned a table set for two. Beautiful crystal glasses and gold charger plates holding gold plate covers awaited them. The scents she caught smelled like beets and something a bit sweeter. Somehow the flowers didn't overwhelm the aroma of the food, and she couldn't wait to see what lay in store for them.

An older gentleman she assumed was the chef appeared next to the table.

"Hello, Jacob. I'd like to introduce you to my friend Sarah Wilson. Sarah, this is Jacob Martin, our fantastic chef." Frank went on to sing Jacob's praises until Jacob interrupted him to seat them.

"All right, Frank. Let's get the lovely lady seated before your food is cold and my head swells too much for me to get back through the door." He laughed as he pulled out her seat for her.

"Thank you, Mr. Martin."

"Please, call me Jacob. I know I'm old, but mister always makes me feel older." He laid her napkin over her lap and lifted her plate cover revealing a lovely appetizer. "I hope you like the roasted beet, pistachio, and pear salad I've prepared."

"Roasted beets are something new for me, but the salad smells wonderful. I'm sure it will be great." Sarah smiled up at him.

"Thank you. I'll go check on the rest of your dinner. Enjoy your salad." He returned her smile, turned, and left the room.

"He seems like a nice man." Sarah picked up her fork and sampled the roasted beet and pear salad. "Oh, this is really good."

Frank beamed. "I told you he's a great chef."

"You did." Hesitating a moment, she then looked Frank in the eye. "Can I ask you something?"

"Of course." A look of concern appeared on his face as he maintained eye contact.

"Why did you really buy this place? You have more than just your business smarts and money tied up in this place."

"Honestly…." A pink tinge crept up his neck.

If she hadn't been staring at him, she'd have missed the slight blush.

He blew out a breath. "I had the best times of my life here…with you. Wanting to share that experience with others is what made me buy the lodge."

His warm palm slid over the back of her hand as his fingers curled around to meet in the center of her palm, sending a thrill up her arm.

Her salad suddenly became more interesting. Not so interesting that she missed the slight smile that curled the corners of his mouth.

Once she finished, Chef Jacob returned with a waiter carrying their dinner in on a large tray.

"I hope you found the salad to your liking, Sarah." He cleared her salad plate from the table and placed her entrée before her.

"The salad was delightful."

He nodded and went on to describe the next course. "This main course is pan-seared scallops on linguine with tomato-cream sauce. The cream gives the slightly tangy sauce a silky-smooth finish. I've also baked fresh French bread to accompany the main dish." He folded back the towel covering the fresh bread, and the warm aroma reached her nose.

"Everything looks absolutely wonderful, Jacob. Your choices are perfect." He nodded when she looked up at him. "Thank you very much for going to all this trouble just for me."

"My pleasure. I'm glad to cook for a pretty face for a change, instead of just that ugly mug." He poked a thumb in Frank's direction.

"Hey, don't forget who signs your paychecks, pal." He cocked an eyebrow with a mock look of shock on his face. "Can you believe the lack of respect I get around here?"

The men's playful banter made her laugh.

"I hope you don't mind, but I called for a bottle of Burgundy to go with your dinner. Now, I'll leave you to your meal. If you need anything, don't hesitate to let me know." He gave her a smile and a slight nod before leaving the room.

"I'm beginning to get the feeling Jacob likes you more than he likes me," Frank teased. "He's barely spoken to me since we sat down."

CHAPTER FIVE

FRANK escorted her back to office where their after dinner coffees and two servings of Chocolate Chunk Bread Pudding were sitting on the occasional table. He settled next to her on sofa and handed her a mug.

The aroma drifted to her nose, and she breathed deep. "You remember how I take it. Thanks." The thought that he cared enough to remember chipped away a little piece of the wall around her heart.

"You're welcome. Are you ready for dessert? I can have Jacob take them back to the kitchen, if you aren't."

"Are you crazy? That smells divine." She toed off her boots and curled her feet up under her, enjoying the dessert and the music playing through the lodge speakers. A knock interrupted the tranquility of the evening.

As Frank opened the door, she saw one of the men from the ski shop.

"Sir, I'm sorry to interrupt, but we have a problem. A skier has gone missing on trail seven. Do you want me to call Search and Rescue?" The young man looked scared to death.

She hoped the skier wasn't injured. Maybe the skier stopped to take a break along the way and whoever he is here with got nervous when he didn't come straight back.

"How long have they been missing?"

"I wasn't on duty when he went out, but the paperwork shows he's been out for several hours."

"Yes, call the guys in. It's dark and everyone should be off the mountain by now. I'll take a run out there, as well. I know the trail." Turning to Sarah, he leaned down, and grasped her hand. "Will you wait for me? I need to do what I can to make sure our missing skier is safe. It shouldn't take me too long. I know these trails like the back of my hand."

"Wouldn't it be better to let Search and Rescue deal with this?" The trails are dangerous at night, and she didn't want something to happen to him.

"I'm trained and the head of our local Search and Rescue. I'll be fine." The corners of his mouth curled up in a soft smile.

"Of course, do what you need to. I'll reacquaint myself with the place while you're out. Be careful, and I hope you find your missing skier unharmed." She stood, entwined their fingers, and gave his hand a gentle squeeze.

"If you decide it's getting too late and want to go home, have someone from the staff call Tom. He'll come back and take you. But I hope you'll wait, I'm not ready to end our time together, yet. I should be back in an hour or two tops. Trail seven is for experienced skiers, but it's not dangerous." He moved closer and pressed his warm lips to her cheek. "Wish me luck."

"I'll be here when you get back." She returned his kiss with a soft one to his lips. "Good luck, Frank. Hurry back."

With a smug smile, he turned and rushed off toward the ski shop.

Wandering out to the main room, she walked over and stood at a window overlooking the lift area.

The sky had grown darker since she'd arrived. Luckily, there wasn't any new snow in the forecast, if the weatherman could be trusted to be accurate.

She watched a group of men assemble at the base of the ski lift. All of them wore the local Search and Rescue safety vests and carried flashlights and lanterns. She sent a prayer out they found the skier and all returned safe and sound.

A couple team members left on snowmobiles. They would

be needed if the skier was injured. They'd need to get him down the trail and to a hospital as quickly as possible.

"Ms. Wilson, my name is Amy. Would you like some company while we wait?"

A lovely young blonde woman joined her at the window.

"Hello, Amy. I'd love some company. Let's sit." She admired the young lady as she sat in one of the wingback chairs nearest the window. "Are you the Amy behind the beautiful flower arrangements around the lodge and in the conference room where Frank and I had dinner?"

"Yes, I'm that Amy. I hope the flowers were a nice addition to your dinner." She sat a little straighter with apparent pride, but the look on her face showed uncertainty.

"The flowers were gorgeous. Thank you." Her gaze kept straying to the window and what lay beyond. The mountain side fought the clock for her attention. Neither would be ignored. She struggled to keep the small talk going. "Is this your first job?"

* * *

TRAIPSING around on the side of this mountain hadn't been part of his plans for the evening.

It was dark and friggin' frigid out there. "Hey, guys, lets split up on this ridge and clear it quicker. Mike, you take North Point, and don't forget to check the game trail on the backside. Joe, take West Branch. I'll check *my* spot. I remember talking to Mr. Miller about wildlife vantage points when his wife and he checked in. He may have gone there, lost track of time, and now can't figure out which way back. We'll meet up in an hour. That should be enough time to check each location and get back before the next storm front moves in."

The guys headed out to search their assigned areas as Frank shined his flashlight around his current location. This slope was well skied, so it wasn't going to be easy to separate any possible lone skiers, but staying to the edge of the pathways would reveal anyone slipping away from the normal route.

He slipped the flashlight into the ring on his backpack and flipped his headlamp back on. Heading down the slope, he allowed his mind to wander while keeping an eye on the edge of the trail.

Would Sarah be at the lodge when he got back? Did she decide to have Tom take her home? Doubt crept in, and he wished he'd let the others handle the search. Leaving her alone tonight was not how he wanted the evening to go. He couldn't catch a break with a baseball mitt.

Sliding his skis to the side, he stopped to check his surroundings. Shining the flashlight at the tree line, his favorite spot was just ahead. A bit farther past the opening to his clearing were ski tracks.

Miller must have realized he'd gone too far and tried cutting over. Taking the path someone's skis had made, Frank followed in the hope the skier wouldn't be far away.

The trees weren't too thick in this section, but they looked a lot bigger and more foreboding in the dark. The tracks continued for at least a mile, weaving around tree trunks as they cut through the snow.

Wood smoke wafted on the breeze. That had to be Miller. *At least he has some skills.* Clicking his headlamp off, he looked around the stand of trees to see if the fire was close. A slight orange glow breached the landscape about two hundred feet ahead. He grabbed his flashlight to light his path.

He moved in slowly in case it wasn't Miller. Once he was past the last row of trees, he called to the figure hunched near a small fire. "Mr. Miller?"

Miller glanced his way and threw his arm up in front of his eyes to block the glare from the flashlight. "Thank God, Mr. Taylor."

"You know this wasn't meant as a camping site."

"I can't say camping was on my list of things to do this week. Busted up my damn ski and blew my knee out in the same crash. Thought I'd rest a bit and try and hike it back to the lodge. Waited a bit too long, it got dark faster than I expected." Miller rubbed around his left knee and flinched when he stroked a little too close to the knee joint. "Wasn't sure what to do, but knew I needed some protection from the weather. A fire was first, then the lovely abode you see behind me.

Frank looked over the man's shoulder and saw a small snow shelter packed around the base of a large pine. "Great job, but how did you do that with a bum knee? That's a lot of work."

"It hurt like hell, but I needed to do it. You dig up energy you never know you have when you're stuck in an emergency situation."

"I'm glad you knew what to do. Most come up here and have no idea." Frank sat down on the log by Miller. "I'll get you back as soon as I rest a bit and get some warmth back into my hands and feet."

Rotating his head from left to right, and then around from shoulder to shoulder he saw the moon disappear. Storm clouds moved in and obstructed his view. *Crap, we've got to get out of here.* "Search and Rescue is out looking so I'll radio the guys and get the sled up here to take you out. We'll be at the lodge in no time." Pulling the radio from inside his jacket, he keyed the mike and got nothing but squealing and squawking. "Shit! Just my luck, I'd grab the screwed up radio." He tried once again only to get dead air.

"Now what do we do, Mr. Taylor?"

"First, call me Frank. Second, I get you back to the lodge. I have a beautiful woman waiting on me, and I know your wife is beside herself with worry for you."

"Nancy is going to kill me. She told me not to come out

here until she could come along. I should have listened." He rubbed at his leg a little more.

"How's the knee? Do you think you can make it back if I build something to pull you on?"

"It still hurts like hell, but I might be able to walk out of here if you help me splint it."

Snow drifted down in fat flakes as he looked for something to support Miller's knee. "Shit, just what we don't need." The storm might delay them, but he wasn't going to sit around waiting for it to pass. He needed to get Miller splinted and in the shelter while he figured out the easiest way to get him down the mountain.

* * *

SARAH and Amy got to know each other better and made small talk until movement outside the window caught their attention.

"Looks like the S and R team is coming in. I hope they were able to find the skier." Amy stood and walked closer to the window.

The Search and Rescue volunteers began to gather back at the base of the ski lift. After several minutes impatiently waiting, they finally filtered into the lodge.

Sarah waited for Frank to come in, but as the other men made their way into the lodge, Frank wasn't among them. "Where is Frank?"

The young man, who came into the office a few hours ago to report the missing skier, looked confused. "He's not here? He's been out of radio contact for a while now. I just thought he'd come back before we did." He turned to the group and asked if anyone had seen Frank.

Once they all reported in with no sign of him she paced to the window, hoping to see him trekking toward the lodge.

"Someone needs to get back out there and find him. He

should have come back with the rest of you. Didn't he have a partner with him? Don't you people search in teams?" She fought to keep the hysterical tone from creeping into her voice. Frank was still out there on the mountain and anything might have happened to him.

"Let's not jump to conclusions. He may have found Miller and is slow coming in, give him a little longer before we rush back out there. Frank knows these trails better than anyone."

Sarah wasn't sure who spoke but knew they were being more logical than her at the moment. She didn't like it though. If something had happened they were wasting valuable time.

"Sarah, come sit down with me. We'll keep an eye out for him from the window. If he isn't back within the hour we'll send a few people out to look for him." Amy turned to the team. "Was there any sign of the skier?"

Someone from the back of the room said, "No, none."

"Frank probably found him, and he's being extra careful coming back. And I bet why he hasn't radioed in is because he grabbed the handset with the funky battery. The replacement hasn't come in yet."

"But wouldn't he have tested the radio first?"

"I'm sure he did, and the radio probably worked. The battery is temperamental. They keep talking about pitching the stupid thing but keep forgetting to actually do it." Amy kept glancing out the window.

If this situation stirred up all the emotions she avoided over the years, did she really want a relationship, to risk losing someone else? Did she want to chance another broken heart?

"So how long have you known Frank, Sarah?" Amy's attention remained on what lay outside.

"All of my life. He's my older brother's best friend." She joined Amy at the window, hoping to see Frank making his way to the lodge. The view to the top of the slope remained empty of human life though. "We lost contact after I married and raised a family. He'd moved on to build his career, and I started writing and raising a son."

"Oh, I didn't know you were married. Where is your husband, if you don't mind my asking?" Her attention now lay fully on Sarah, awaiting her answer.

"I don't mind. He died five years ago after a car accident left him in a coma." Sarah continued to gaze out the window, unseeing of the view before her.

"I'm sorry. I didn't mean to bring up painful memories." Amy ducked her head and stared at the floor.

"Don't apologize, life happened and went on, whether I wanted it to or not." They needed to get out and look for Frank. He might be hurt and slowly freezing to death while they sat chatting. "We have to get them out looking for Frank and their missing skier."

"Hang on, I'll go talk to a couple team members I know and see if they have any plans on going back out." Amy walked away, and Sarah returned to staring out the window.

The night moved on but not for Sarah, hers appeared to come to a standstill. She and Frank had just found each other, and even with all her doubts she wasn't ready to lose him again.

While not well endowed with patience, she did have plenty of practice distracting herself. *Now to find something to do— anything to keep from obsessing about Frank not returning with the rest of them.*

"Sorry, Sarah, no one is ready to go back out yet. I tell you what, would you mind helping me with something while we wait?" Amy stood next to her with an expectant look on her face.

"Sure, anything to keep from driving myself crazy. What do you need me to do?" She turned from the window and faced Amy.

"I'm going to check the water in the vases and remove any

dead flowers. Thought you might like some busy work too. When we're done with this maybe you can help me come up with some new holiday arrangements. We'll keep busy as long as we can." Amy led her to the coolers where the flowers were stored.

There were several pump canisters used to water the various plants and cut flower arrangements placed throughout the lodge. Following Amy's lead, Sarah grabbed one of the remaining canisters and worked the opposite side of the room from Amy.

She plucked out brown, wilted flowers and greenery, replacing stems with fresh cuts from a cart Amy pulled from the cooler. The sound of a grandfather clock striking ten somewhere in the lodge made her look up and see the young man from earlier coming toward her.

Amy rushed toward him. "Mike…."

So that's his name.

Sarah didn't hear anything else said, but saw Mike shake his head no. Apparently, Frank and the skier still weren't back. She met up with them in the center of the hall. The flowers and arrangements forgotten.

"Have Frank and the missing skier made it back yet? Sorry, I never asked your name."

"I'm Mike, and it has been hectic, so it's understandable. I'm sorry, but Frank isn't back yet. I was going to take Tim and Joe with me to check out a few places we know he goes to when he gets a chance to go skiing, but we have to wait. The flurries the news forecasted has turned into a bit more of a storm."

"You can't leave him out there. Someone has to go get him. What if he's hurt?" A pain near her heart made her press her hand to her chest. They needed to find Frank now.

A couple men approached their little group and spoke in whispers only Mike could hear.

"The guys aren't going to leave Frank out there. They said we can get where we split off from him and back even with the snow falling. The storm shouldn't be much of a hindrance as long as a wind doesn't pick up. We're leaving as soon as we can get geared up."

"Thank you, Mike. Please be careful, and bring everyone back safe."

Amy followed them back to the main room and approached one of the other men suited up to go out. He was obviously one of the men Mike mentioned. She hugged the man before he walked out with Mike and the other fellow.

She didn't want to be a voyeur so she walked over to the panoramic window. *Where are you Frank? Please come back.* She watched the room reflected in the window. She couldn't stop thinking something awful happening to him. They'd lost so much time not staying in contact over the last several years. She wanted the chance she didn't take all those years ago.

Most of the guests had gone to their rooms, but one woman sat by the fireplace, quietly watching the comings and goings of the staff. *She must be the skier's wife.* Amy came into view, carrying a tray with several mugs and two carafes.

"Would you like to join us, Sarah? This is Mrs. Miller. Her husband is the skier they are out looking for." Amy set the tray down on the coffee table in front of Mrs. Miller.

"Please, call me Nancy."

"Hello, Nancy, I'm Amy, and this is Sarah. She's Frank's girlfriend."

Sarah bit her tongue when Amy introduced her as Frank's girlfriend. The assumption wasn't important in the bigger scheme of things.

He seemed to be interested in a relationship from all the little hints throughout their evening. But her doubts crept back in. Could she open herself up to that kind of commitment, the kind of pain loss can cause? The emotional complications a relationship carried was something she needed to think about, if he pursued more than a friendship after tonight.

"Sarah…Sarah! Earth to Sarah!"

She jolted back to reality with Amy calling her name and gripping her shoulder.

"Sorry, what were you saying?"

"I just asked if you'd like a cup of coffee or hot chocolate." Amy had already poured Nancy a mug and sat patiently waiting on her to decide what she wanted.

"Coffee, black, please." Her gaze traveled back out the window to the mountain side.

"Watching the slope won't get them to come back any quicker. I've tried that technique all evening." Nancy gave her a knowing smile when she looked at her. "I've tried keeping busy, but nothing keeps my mind from wandering to what might have happened, then on to never seeing my husband again." Her voice cracked with emotion.

"I'm sure they will find him and bring him back to you, safe and sound." Sarah's gaze wandered back out the window. *Frank has to come back.*

A comforting weight fell over Sarah's shoulders.

A sympathetic smile graced Amy's face, as she straightened a quilt over Sarah's shoulders and then moved on to give Nancy a blanket, too.

"How long have you known Frank?"

"Since we were kids, Nancy. He's my brother's best friend. We actually came here on family vacations together. He told me that's why he bought this place. He wanted to preserve it and offer the same type of safe family vacations we experienced." Sarah's heart squeezed when she thought back on all that Frank had shared with her over the past several days.

"You've loved him for a long time, haven't you?" Amy studied her as she turned to answer.

"Yes. Life happened and we drifted in opposite directions, but we recently found each other again." Maybe if she stared long enough and prayed hard enough, Frank would magically appear on the slope soon. Who was she kidding, Frank still meant the world to her. He had to come back, she couldn't lose him again, not now.

Nancy joined her at the window. "The snow isn't letting up, is it? I know you're watching and praying. I have been too, but you can do the same from the couch. Come with me and try to relax for a little bit."

"Okay, thanks, Nancy. Well, I've told you about Frank and me, how long have you been married?" She took a seat on one of the sofas closest to the massive stone fireplace while Nancy and Amy sat on the matching sofa facing her.

While the women sat and talked, Sarah found out Nancy's husband's name was Jerry, and they were celebrating their tenth wedding anniversary. Amy and Joe, the young man she saw her hug earlier, had only been dating for a couple months.

As if someone had flipped a switch, Amy and Nancy grew quiet.

She fought a yawn and lost as the grandfather clock next to fireplace struck the half hour. Sleep crept up, making her eyelids heavy. She tucked her feet up under her and laid her head on the sofa arm.

* * *

"SARAH. Sarah, honey, wake up." Her soft cheek warmed his fingers as he caressed her face. He hadn't meant to take so long. If only they'd removed the faulty battery instead of trying to make it last until the new one came in.

This was not the impression he'd wanted to make on her. Maybe he had a chance, if she didn't run back to her cabin once she awoke. He shouldn't have gone looking for Miller. There were plenty of volunteers who knew the slopes just as well as he did.

"Sarah, I'm back." He brushed her hair back off her forehead and cleared the soft strands from over her eyes.

"Frank!" Sarah jumped up and straight into his arms. "Thank God, you're safe."

Her body was warm from sleep and the heat seeped into him, chasing away the chill from being out in the snow so long. They fit together, as if she were meant to be part of him. As her arms tightened around his shoulders, he wrapped his around her.

"You're not hurt, are you?" Sarah pulled away and ran her hands over his shoulders, arms, chest, and back. "Where have you been? Did you find Nancy's husband? Is he okay—"

"Whoa, slow down. One question at a time. I'm fine. Jerry is back with Nancy with only a bum knee. Tom is on his way to take them into town so he can see the doctor.

"He went searching for one of the areas he heard us talking about and broke one of his skis. After trying to fix it, he realized it was getting dark, and then he wasn't sure how to get back. Luckily, he knows what he's doing. He'd taken an emergency blanket and had started a fire. Sorry I took so long getting back, with him only having one ski it wasn't an easy trek. And it didn't help that I grabbed the radio with the screwed up battery." Having someone worry about him was nice, but he certainly hadn't meant to scare her.

"Thankfully everyone is safe. Amy told me about the radio's battery, and she was confident you had grabbed that one. Guess I should have trusted her intuition or whatever it was." She smiled while looking over his shoulder. Turning, he saw Amy with her boyfriend as she looked up, smiled back at Sarah, and waved before leaving with Joe.

"I'm glad Amy stayed and kept you company. I'm also sorry I left you in the first place. I truly thought it would be a quick retrieval and return." He sat back on the couch and pulled her into his arms again.

"I'm just glad you and everyone else made it back with no serious injuries. Now, please throw out that battery." She sighed and settled in against his side, laying her head on his shoulder.

"It went in the recycle bin the minute I came in." The tropical scent of her shampoo tickled his nose when he rested his cheek against the top of her head. He was happy to see she hadn't called Tom to take her home when he didn't come back.

He pulled her back into his embrace and reclined on the couch. With her body heat and the quilt to warm him, he was nodding off until Amy squeezed his shoulder.

"You need to go upstairs and get some real rest." She winked and walked away.

"She's right, you need to go to bed." Sarah tilted her head back to look him in the face.

"Do you want me to take you home?" He dreaded her reply. The last thing he wanted was to let her go now.

"Are you kidding? You've just spent hours out there freezing your butt off. The last thing you need to do is drive me home. This place is big enough I'm sure we can find a place for me to sleep. You need to rest." She smiled, palming his cheek. "Honey, you really need to sleep, you look like hell."

"Gee, thanks. I can't catch a break today. My chef likes my date better than me, the guy who signs his paychecks, and my girl thinks I look like shit." Frank tensed a bit. He hoped she either missed his slip altogether or took it for a joke. He hadn't even broached the subject of a relationship with her yet.

"Your girl, huh? I don't remember saying you looked like shit. What I said was, you looked like hell. You'll always be one of the most handsome men I've ever known, no matter how tired you look."

Her hand slipped from his cheek to the back of his neck

and pulled him down for a kiss. Her soft lips crushed his, surprising him. The depth of her passion rushing through him fed his as he crushed her to him and slid his tongue between her lips to explore the warm cavern of her mouth. Her tongue danced with his before he pulled back and stood.

"Come with me." He pulled her to her feet and led her to his living area on the third floor.

Once they were through the door, he kicked it shut and pulled her back into his arms.

"Frank—" He slipped his finger across her lips.

"The bed is big enough for the both of us, and nothing will happen that you don't want to." He pulled her into his bedroom and rummaged through a drawer for a pair of drawstring sweats and a t-shirt for her. "Here, the bathroom is through there. Slip into those and we'll get some sleep."

Confusion clouded her eyes and the expression on her face as he pushed her to the bathroom. "Go on."

When she closed the door, he slid into his flannel pajama pants and long sleeve thermal shirt. The next few hours were going to be rougher than tonight's rescue, but he wasn't going to rush things. *I'm not going to risk it and scare her away.*

She entered the room carrying her clothes.

"Here, we can hang those in the closet." He took his time pulling hangers out and putting the clothes away.

Closing the closet door, he turned to see her staring at him. "You're procrastinating. It's not a problem if you rather I slept on the couch."

"No way. I'm not putting you on the couch. Come here." Her body fit to his as he pressed her to him. "Sorry, I'm just trying really hard to get my head right. You drive me crazy."

"Sorry." Her hands roamed over his back, sending desire spiraling through every cell in his body.

"Nothing for you to be sorry for. It's a good thing, hon." He chuckled as he pulled her hands from around him. "Let's go to bed."

As he drew back the blanket and sheet, he wondered if this was in any way a good idea. Having her all to himself for almost a week had been a hard lesson in patience. Would having her in his bed be a temptation he could deny? Once he made her comfortable, he walked around and climbed in on the other side. He pulled the blankets up over his body and settled in, facing her. He propped up on his elbow, to watch her in the moonlight. "God, you're beautiful."

"Flattery will get you everywhere, big boy." She laughed as he stammered for something to say. She turned on her side to face him.

"I didn't mean that as a joke. I'm serious. You are a beautiful woman." He lifted his arm to her and kissed her forehead when she obliged him. As he moved so she could lay her head on his chest, she left a soft kiss over his heart before finally laying down.

Thank God for shirts. Not sure I'd survive the night if her lips actually touched my skin. Lips were one thing but anywhere else was another story.

Her breathing evened out, and when he tilted his head to look down at her face, he found she'd fallen asleep.

She snuggled in closer and lifted her knee, sliding her thigh across his groin. He heaved a sigh of relief she wasn't aware of the state he was in as they lay there in each other's arms.

He dropped his head onto the pillow and squeezed his eyes shut. *It's going to be a long night.*

* * *

THE combination of a warm body shifting next to him, brushing skin on skin, and the sunlight breaking through his eyelids woke Frank before he wanted.

A contented grin spread across his face when he breathed in the light tropical scent of Sarah's shampoo again and found her hand had crept up his shirt during the night. He could get used to her being next to him every morning. Now, all he had to do was convince her they were a great idea. First, he needed make a call.

He grabbed his cell phone off the nightstand and slipped out of bed. The angel under the blankets burrowed further into the bedding but remained asleep. The bathroom door *snicked* shut quietly, and he dialed Joe and Amy.

"Hey guys, how's it going?"

"I'm going to need a couple hours. Amy's on her way back to help you stall her."

"Thanks, Joe, do you need me to send someone out to help you finish?"

"No, what's left is just busy work. I can handle it."

"Okay, I'll let you get back to it. Thanks again."

"Sure thing, Frank. I'll call when I've got everything cleaned up. Talk to you soon."

As Frank disconnected the call, sounds from the other room caught his attention. Now, he needed to find something to take her mind off going home for a few hours. His surprise wasn't quite ready.

Walking out of the bathroom, he slid his phone back on the nightstand, and caught Sarah fighting with the blankets in her sleep.

He climbed back into bed and freed her from the tangled mess she'd created. She moved into his embrace and calmed back down into a restful sleep.

When he relaxed and inhaled her familiar coconut scent, his phone rang. He scrambled to answer it before the noise woke Sarah.

"Hey, boss. Would you two like some coffee and breakfast?" Amy's voice was smiling as she spoke.

"Coffee would be great, Amy. Thanks." When he turned toward Sarah, her gaze met his. *Wow.* This woman still resided in the part of his heart Janet was never able to reach.

"One more reason I love my staff. Would you like some coffee and some breakfast?"

"Coffee sounds wonderful." She shifted again and tucked in closer, as if she was trying to avoid the sun.

Frank had no problem with her cuddling into him. He liked having her tucked under his arm, she fit perfectly.

"Ooh, and some of that fantastic dessert from last night, if Jacob has any left."

"I'm sure he does. I doubt he made less than twelve serving, probably more."

Jacob chose that moment to make himself known in the background, so Frank hit the speaker.

Amy repeated the conversation, and Jacob confirmed. "Of course I have some chocolate chunk bread pudding for my next favorite lady."

"Next favorite?" Sarah pretended to pout.

"If I said you were my favorite and it got back to my wife, I'd be sleeping with the chickens."

"In that case, I'll accept next favorite." The smile on her face made her look like she did when they were younger.

"Much appreciated, milady." Jacob's chuckle was loud and clear over the connection.

"Okay, boss, I'll have everything for you as quick as I can. See you in a few."

"Thanks for everything, Amy."

He ended the call and turned back to Sarah, who still laid wrapped around his waist. "I have another surprise for you today. I wanted to do it last night after dinner but, of course, I had to delay it."

"Now what have you done, Frank?" Her left eyebrow cocked up. The smile she tried to compress leaked out as she shook her head.

"Let's move into the dining room. Amy will be here with

the coffee shortly." He forced himself out of bed, and she grasped the hand he held out to her, allowing him to help her stand.

The closet stood open with his robe hanging on the back of the door. He grabbed it and wrapped it around her shoulders. "You do realize today is Christmas Eve, right?" He went to the door and opened it for Amy, who wheeled a small cart through the doorway.

"Yes, so what?"

"Well, you'll just have to see when we get back to your place." He winked at her as she sat forward when Amy reached the table.

"Good morning, you two. I can't believe you two almost fell asleep on the couch of all places." Amy sat the tray with the coffee and mugs on the table once he took a seat across from Sarah.

"Exhaustion hit me like a Mack truck. The moment she cuddled into my side and her warmth soaked in, I was done." Her cheeks turned pink, and he squeezed her hand. "No reason to be embarrassed, Sarah. That was a compliment." He picked up her hand and kissed the soft skin of her knuckles before releasing her to pour them each a cup of coffee.

"Thank you for keeping me busy last night, Amy. It helped more than you know." Sarah stood and hugged Amy.

"Glad I was here to help. I know waiting on them to return was driving me crazy, I could only imagine what you were going through." Amy stepped toward the door. "Time for me to get back to work. I hope to see you again."

"I'll make sure of it." Frank waved and turned back to Sarah. "I'm going to take a quick shower."

"I'll explore a little, if you don't mind. I haven't seen your home yet." She took the hand he offered and carried her coffee mug in the other.

"My area isn't quite as fancy as downstairs, it's comfortable though." He showed her around the rest of the area a bit, and then entered his study.

"Wow, Frank, you did a great job up here. This is lovely." Why was he not surprised when she stopped in front of his floor-to-ceiling bookshelves?

"See, I told you I needed to bring those books from my office back up here. Make yourself at home, I'm going to jump in the shower real quick, and then we'll head to your place." He grabbed a change of clothes, walked into the bathroom, and jumped in the shower.

God, what if she doesn't like the way they decorated her house? He should have found a way to clear it with her first. She might be offended. Great, he hadn't thought of that. Why hadn't he stopped to think this all through?

The warm water flowing over his head didn't help clear his doubt. All he could do was cross his fingers and hope she liked what he did for her. One could be undone, the other couldn't be undone or returned.

After shutting the water off, he exited the shower, and dried off. She'd waited enough for a lifetime last night, he wasn't going to make her wait again so he dressed in a hurry, leaving his hair wet.

When he entered the dining room, she sat at the table, already dressed.

"I'm finished. You can have the bathroom. There's a fresh toothbrush on the counter."

"Thank you."

As she closed the door behind her, he grabbed his phone and called Joe. Joe said he'd call when he was done, but he should be back to the lodge by now.

"Hey, Frank, all done. Just put the last box back in the garage. All's clear to bring the lady home for your surprise."

"You're the best, Joe. Remind to give you a raise."

Joe chuckled. "Well, you'd have to hire me before you

could give me a raise."

"Oh, that's right, you work for Amy." Frank laughed, then looked up and saw Sarah standing in front of him.

"Hey, gotta go. Thanks again, Joe."

He disconnected and slipped his phone into his pocket. "Are you ready to head home?"

"Sure. You're really excited about whatever you did, aren't you?" She laughed at him.

"I think I'm more worried you won't like it." Frank grabbed his keys and wallet before holding the door open for her.

"I'm sure I'll love whatever it is. Don't worry so much. As long as you didn't paint my house bright pink, we'll probably be okay." She squeezed his hand and looked up at him with a smile that warmed his worried heart.

They stopped in his office and grabbed their coats. He helped her into hers and threw his on as they headed out to his truck.

Helping her into his vehicle, he couldn't wait to see her face when they pulled up to her house. He wondered how many Christmases she hadn't celebrated since her husband's death but wouldn't ask. Bad memories surfaced enough over the past several days, they didn't need any more.

She turned on the radio and they sang along with the Christmas carols playing. She could at least carry a note. He couldn't carry a tune to save his life, but they had fun, no matter how off-key either one sang.

"Okay, time to close your eyes. You can't open them until I say." He looked over and made sure she did as he told her.

"If I must." She smiled and covered her eyes with her hands.

The truck bounced down the driveway as he drove toward her house. Greenery and ribbons hung on the windowsills and around the banister on the porch. The team did a great job with the decorations. The tree he had ordered was sitting on the porch ready to go in the house if she wanted it.

He stopped the truck and slid the gearshift to park, staring straight ahead. "Okay, you can open your eyes now."

She was quiet so long he thought for sure she hated what they had done. He took a deep breath and exhaled slowly before looking over at her. What he saw surprised him. She sat there with her mouth hanging open and tears brimming. "I'm sorry, Sarah. I can call Amy to bring the guys out and take it all down. I just thought it would be a nice thing to do for you."

She didn't say anything, only closed her mouth and climbed out of the truck. He opened his door and stepped out, meeting her in front of the house. When he was within reach of her, she threw herself into his arms.

Hmmm…twice in as many days. I could get to liking this as long as it isn't because I've upset her.

"I love it. Thank you so much for thinking of doing all this." Her warm breath on his neck made him think of having her in his arms all night. He wished to have her there every night from this day on, but that would have to wait. His wants didn't matter at the moment. He had other surprises in store for her before he could even think about moving them into a committed relationship.

"*Shew!* I thought you hated it. You were quiet for so long." He hugged her and kissed the top of her head.

"No, I could never hate something this beautiful. The house hasn't been decorated for Christmas in years. I'd forgotten how nice everything looks against the snow." She leaned back and looked at her house again. "You even bought a tree?"

"I thought it might be nice to decorate one together." Relief rushed through him as a smile bloomed on her face.

CHAPTER SIX

SHE grabbed him by the hand and pulled him to the house while she dug her keys out with her other hand. "The decorations are in totes up in the attic. Will you bring the tree in, please?"

"Sure, then we'll get the decorations out." He reached into the top of the tree and grabbed the trunk.

"The stand was thoughtful. Now the tree is ready to decorate."

"I wish I could take credit for it, but that must have been Amy. I hadn't thought of the tree needing to settle before we decorated." He smirked as he followed her into the house, bringing the tree along with him.

She directed him to the window to the left of the front door. "Let me move the chest out from in front of the window, and we can set the tree up there out of the way. And this way it can be seen from outside when we turn the lights on tonight."

Shocked, he stumbled as he crossed the threshold when he heard her say 'when *we* turn the lights on tonight.'

"Are you okay? Watch your step, you're going to hurt yourself."

Her laughter made him smile and laugh at himself.

To distract himself from over-thinking what she'd said, he set the tree in place and spent the next several minutes finding the best side to display to the room. "How does this side look? Any large holes between branches?"

"That side looks terrific, Frank. Thank you so much for thinking of this. I've ignored the holidays for too long and forgotten how much I love Christmas."

Warm arms wrapped around him from behind. Her head rested on his back for a moment before he turned in her arms and wrapped her in a strong embrace. "It's my pleasure. I know what it's like to forget the things you once loved when you feel so alone." He rested his head on top of hers when she tucked her head under his chin.

After a few comfortable moments, she leaned back to look him in the eye.

"We aren't alone anymore. I'm glad you came to my door when your truck was stuck in the snow. I've missed you without even realizing you were what I was missing. Does that make sense?" One side of her mouth curved up in a half-smile.

"More than you realize." He tilted his head and did what he'd been longing to do since she revealed she loved his surprise. He pressed his lips to hers in a gentle meshing of lips, but the moment she kissed him back a dam burst and his emotions took over, deepening the kiss. The soft moans coming from her encouraged him to continue.

Her lips molded to his, her body's curves fit to his, to him they were perfection together. Her lips parted the slightest bit, and he slid his tongue into her warm mouth. His knees trembled as her tongue slid across his. What was it about this woman that reduced him to the emotional equivalent of a teenager? Was it because they had history? Whatever caused it, he was glad he'd found her and didn't know what he would do if she walked away from him after this.

Christmas lay just hours away, and with that thought he broke their kiss. Laying his forehead against hers, he waited until he caught his breath. "Let's get the tree decorated before it gets dark."

Her grin grew when he pushed back, and he knew she didn't miss the flush that rose up his neck. He could feel the heat rise inch by inch.

"Okay, but only if you promise we can continue this later."
She winked at him then turned and headed down the hallway.
He smiled watching her pull down the door that hid the access
to the attic.

"Let me grab the boxes. Are they marked with Christmas
or anything?" He listened to her as he climbed the ladder.

"No, but you'll know when you see them, they're all green
totes with red lids. You'll also see black totes with orange lids.
Bet you can't guess what's in those." Her laughter filtered up
through the opening.

"Oh, let's guess, Valentine's Day?"

"Ha, ha, smart aleck. Just grab the Christmas stuff and let's
get this tree decorated so we can get back to the fun stuff."

"Ouch, that hurt. You don't think decorating the tree with
me will be fun?" The boxes slid easily to the attic opening.
When everything they needed rested on the main floor, he
closed the access door and helped take the totes to the living
room.

She laid out the lights, and he tested them to make sure
they all worked. They worked well as a team stringing the long
strands of lights on the tree. Next, the round colored balls
were hung on the individual branches, then the shaped
ornaments. She had candy canes and tinsel to go on once he'd
strung the garland. "Why do you have both the garland and
tinsel? Isn't that a little overkill?"

"Have you ever seen a tree without tinsel? They seem so
unfinished without the added sparkle. Plus, it's my tree and I
want both." Her small pink tongue darted out from between
her lips as she stuck it out at him.

"Did you just stick your tongue out at me? How old are
you, eight?" He shook his head and laughed when she did it
again. "We need to talk about when that is appropriate."

"Oh, I know exactly when to use it." She wiggled her
eyebrows and laughter burst out of her.

"You're a nut." She was so much fun, exactly the way he remembered her all those years ago. He laughed so much and so long his face and stomach hurt.

The backside of the tree needed some tinsel. He squeezed between the tree and the window, tossing small handfuls of tinsel over the ends of the branches. Sarah had grown silent. "Sarah?" He peeked around the tree to see her looking down at her hands.

He came to her side. "Sarah, honey, is everything all right?"

"Promise me you won't go out on the slopes without a partner again, please. Last night was awful. The waiting, wondering, and worrying forced me back to the night of Rick's accident. I don't want to live through that again." The tears in her eyes nearly broke his heart.

"I promise, Sarah, I won't put you through a night like last night again." He pulled her into his arms and held her tight. "I promise I won't go back out without a partner. Going alone was a stupid thing to do, and I know better. I was just in such a hurry. We covered more ground splitting up, and sure of where he'd went, which I was correct about." He slid his fingers through her hair and palmed the back of her head. As he massaged her scalp with his fingertips, her body softened and relaxed into him.

"Let's make dinner. We can light the tree once we've finished eating and clean up." She released him and led him into the kitchen. "I have beef stew in the freezer. We can heat it up, and I'll mix up some homemade biscuits and get them in the oven while the stew is warming."

"You're going to spoil me, woman. All this home cooking is going to make me fat and lazy." He stuck out his stomach and flopped down on a kitchen chair.

"I'm sure I can come up with ways to keep you active enough so you don't become fat and lazy." She winked and continued gathering the butter, flour, and other ingredients to get the biscuits started. She also pulled the stew from the freezer and started warming it on the stove.

He stood and walked over to the counter, where he watched her measure out flour and other ingredients, and dump them into a large bowl. "Is there anything I can do?"

"Want to stock the firewood and get a fire going?"

How could he refuse? Having her cuddle up to him in front of a roaring fire sounded like the perfect evening. "Coming right up." There was plenty of wood stacked to the right, and the size of the fireplace made building a nice fire easy. Flames danced in the hearth in no time.

The aromas wafting in from the kitchen lured him back. She was looking into the oven when he reached the kitchen doorway and stopped short. How had he ever been stupid enough to walk away from her? The only explanation he could come up with was he'd been young and dumb.

Well, not anymore. She's mine, and I won't screw up again.

Her beauty had only grown over the years. He'd fallen hard for her back in school, and he'd ran away to college to avoid his feelings and to avoid revealing those feelings for his best friend's sister. *Dumbass, you should have bared your soul.* He would spend the rest of their lives making up for his lack of courage back then, if she'd let him.

"Hey, you, perfect timing. Everything is ready. Help me move the food to the table, please?" She handed him the dish of warm stew, and carried the biscuits to the table.

"Sure, this smells wonderful. I can't wait to taste it." His mouth was watering. *You'd think I haven't eaten in days.* "Where did you learn to cook like this? I don't remember your mom cooking meals completely from scratch much."

"Cookbooks and cooking shows on cable." She laughed as she broke open a biscuit and slathered it with butter. "Hope you aren't worried about your cholesterol. I don't buy margarine, only real butter."

He took the biscuit from her. "It would be akin to blasphemy to use anything but real butter on these homemade biscuits." The buttery goodness melted in his mouth. "Mmmm. This has to be the best I've ever had."

"Thank you, I'm glad you like them." She smiled as he tried the stew.

"This stew is great too. You know I'm going to have to marry you now. There's no way I can go back to fast food or microwave dinners."

Sarah laughed. "Fast food and microwave dinners, huh? I'll be sure to tell Jacob what you think of his food."

"Oh God, no. Please, don't do that. He'll never cook me another meal." He clutched his chest, exaggerating his horror at her words to make her laugh more. He loved the sound of her laughter and hoped he'd have many chances to hear it.

With the meal finished and the kitchen clean, he sat on the sofa in front of the fireplace in the living room. He'd left plenty of room beside him for her to snuggle up with him or leave a comfortable distance between them if she so chose.

Thankfully, she sat next to him, settling her feet up on the other side of her as she tucked in under his arm.

"This is how Christmas Eve should be."

"Yes, it's almost perfect." A sad, faraway look filled her eyes while she stared into the fire. Something in her tone told him she was thinking of her son.

"Speaking of perfect, can I get your house key for tomorrow?"

She looked up at him with a confused look on her face. "Why do you need my house key?"

"I need to be able to bring in your Christmas gift." He rubbed small circles on her shoulder with his fingertips while he prayed she didn't ask too many questions.

"You aren't going to stay tonight?"

"I'd love to stay, if that's what you want. But I still need a key. I can't pick up your gift until dawn tomorrow."

"What have you done, Frank?"

"Nope, that's all I'm going to say about it, so don't ask any more questions." Her arm slipped across his waist and he tightened his hold of her for a quick squeeze.

"Okay, but I don't have anything for you. I haven't exactly been able to get out shopping." Her head rested on his shoulder and her forehead lay against his neck.

"I'm not worried about a gift, having you back in my life is gift enough." Her eyes sparkled with firelight when he palmed her jaw and tilted her head up. The silkiness of her skin and the shape of her lips distracted him for a moment. Not long enough for him to forget he planned to kiss her well enough to curl her toes, though.

Her eyelashes tickled his lip as he kissed each closed eyelid, before lightly brushing his lips across hers. When he saw the look of contentment on her face, and her tongue slide across her lower lip, he couldn't hold back, he crushed her to him and sucked her bottom lip into his mouth. Warm hands slid up under his shirt when he released her lip and slid his tongue into her mouth.

She tensed for a minute in his arms and he backed off the kiss. Did he screw up and push too hard or did she just not like the kiss?

"Santa will be coming soon. Let's go to bed. I have a surprise of my own." She stood and tugged on his hand. The small smile on her face turned into a deliciously wicked grin.

He gladly followed, relieved his line of questioning appeared to be completely wrong.

* * *

"MERRY Christmas, darling. I'm glad someone decorated the house. You wouldn't have done it yourself. Please, get back into life. Enjoy the holidays and the people in your life." Rick sat on the porch in early

morning light. She sat in her rocker next to his, without a coat, but then this was a dream after all. She didn't have to worry about getting cold or frostbite here.

"Merry Christmas, Rick. It's weird saying that to you after all these years." She looked over and smiled at him. "This view is beautiful. I'd forgotten how wonderful the mornings are."

"You need to take the time to remember. Life is too short to ignore the beauty of the small things." He brushed her hand, but she couldn't really feel it, just the sensation of air movement across her skin.

"I will. I've missed out on so much since you passed away, but not anymore. I'm going to enjoy every minute of the time I have left."

"I hope you enjoy your gift. It was a joint effort." He winked and wafted away, replaced by the smell of coffee.

* * *

SUNLIGHT leaked between her eyelids as she realized the smell of coffee wasn't part of her dream. Frank must have gotten up early and started the coffeemaker. She grabbed her robe and headed for the kitchen, only to find the place empty.

Once she'd poured herself a cup of coffee, she walked to the picture window and looked out at the snow-covered meadow.

Frank's reflection appeared over her shoulder a few minutes later.

"Hey, beautiful, Merry Christmas." Frank nuzzled her neck.

"Merry Christmas." In his arms she was content, something she hadn't felt since Rick.

"I have one more surprise for you. Wait here." Frank left and went out the front door.

She moved back to the coffeemaker and refreshed her cup. Opening the cupboard, she pulled out a mixing bowl to make pancakes for breakfast.

"Do you have enough for an idiot of a son?"

She looked up to see her handsome brown-eyed son

standing in the kitchen doorway. "Chris!" Rushing around the counter, she ran to Chris and threw her arms around him. "Oh my God, you have no idea how happy I am."

"I'm sorry I've such an idiot for so long. Believe me or not, I think Dad has been haunting me." He looked at her as if he expected her to laugh at him.

"I know. He was haunting me as well. Guess he got tired of us both being stupid." She hugged him again, and then stepped back. "Let me make us some breakfast, and we can talk more over pancakes."

"Sounds great, Mom. I've missed your cooking."

Frank stood behind Chris and she waved him over.

She stepped back to allow room for him to join them. "Frank, this is my son—"

Chris interrupted her. "We've met over the phone, then finally in person at the airport early this morning."

"Chris was the gift you said you couldn't pick up until dawn this morning, isn't he?" Tears came to her eyes as Frank nodded. She couldn't believe he'd contacted her son and helped convince him to come home for Christmas after all these years. She wrapped her arms around Frank. "Thank you," she whispered.

He smiled as she excused herself to start breakfast, leaving Chris and Frank to get to know each other better.

A movement outside the window made her step back and look at the beautiful blue sky. She saw the face of her late husband fade into the distance. "Merry Christmas, Rick. Something tells me you had everything to do with Frank getting stuck and stranded here too." A smile crept across her face. "Thanks for the wonderful Christmas gifts."

She lifted her coffee mug in a toast and turned to watch her new life begin.

The End

AUTHOR

ARIANA Gaynor spends her time in central Ohio, loving her kids, her dog Shadow, and her lizard Izzy. Once the house is quiet and the work is over, she spends her time writing. She loves helping other authors. Sewing, crocheting, and knitting are a few of the hobbies she enjoys.

www.ingramcontent.com/pod-product-compliance
Lightning Source LLC
Chambersburg PA
CBHW022048170626
46808CB00003B/1406